A TIME
AND A PLACE

Authors previous Publications

The Weed
A Selection of Poems
A Pause in Time

A TIME
AND A PLACE

A COLLECTION OF SHORT STORIES TO STRETCH YOUR IMAGINATION TO THE LIMITS, SOME FACT, SOME FICTION, ON A VARIATION OF DIFFERENT THEMES.

by
Raymond Thomas Edwards

First published in 2010 by
Raymond Thomas Edwards

© Copyright 2010
Raymond Thomas Edwards

The right of Raymond Thomas Edwards to be identified as
the author of this work has been asserted by him in
accordance with the Copyright, Designs and Patents 1988

All Rights Reserved
No reproduction, copy or transmission of this publication
may be made without written permission. No paragraph of
this publication may be reproduced, copied or transmitted
save with written permission or in accordance with the
provisions of the Copyright Act 1956 (as amended)

ISBN : 0 9542716 3 7

Printed and bound in Great Britain by:
Willow Design and Print Ltd
Loverock House
Brettell Lane, Brierley Hill
West Midlands. DY5 3JS

All of the places, characters and events in this book
are fictitious.
Any resemblance to actual persons, living or dead
is purely coincidental

CONTENTS

1.	Catherine McGuire	1
2.	Demidrogs	12
3.	Echoes from the Grave	24
4.	Enemy from the Sea	36
5.	Old Nellie the Steam Engine	46
6.	Legend of the Little Red Hen	57
7.	My Journal	62
8.	My Old Gang of Long Ago	73
9.	Orchids of the Moon	82
10.	Grandma's Birthday Present	105
11.	The Amorous Cavalier	115
12.	The Devil Cat	126
13.	The Winged Dog Mites of Bhyktor	142

Catherine McGuire

The court room was silent like a grave as Lydia McGuire gave her own account of her late mother's last few months of her life leading up to her suicide. She sat facing the coroner and members of the bench, as the inquest into her late mothers death was being investigated. Her long black curly hair hung down her back tied with a black ribbon; there wasn't a strand out of place. She wore dark glasses hiding a very beautiful face, which at this moment in time was badly bruised following a fight with her late mother. Her trim shapely figure fitted into her dark green two piece suit like a glove. She was truly a very beautiful and attractive woman.

Speaking in a quiet and very refined voice, she began telling her heart-rendering story, her sophisticated and polished accent explaining in detail the circumstances leading to her late mother's demise.

"My two younger sisters and I", pointing at two young ladies sitting in the courtroom, "lived the earlier parts of our lives on the east coast of England. Our mother received a bang on the head due to a fall and this resulted in a temporary loss of memory, I can only say what happened next, shaped our lives for the future. The injury my mother had received made her aggressive and she and my father were constantly bickering. In a fit of rage one day my father decided to up stakes and move to the north west coast of England dragging us all behind him kicking and screaming leaving our friends and relations behind, his ambition being to expand his components empire across all the counties of England. There my father set about building new factories and recruiting a new work force to build spare parts for cars, machines, aircraft, and domestic appliances.

I remember at the time having words with my mother over it, my complaint being, I was twenty years old just finished college and now was about to be dragged all the way over to the north west coast of England,

"I'm not going", I said bitterly.

What followed next sent the shivers racing down my spine. She stood up and came walking over to me and gazed into my eyes. It was like staring into the eyes of the Medusa, any minute expecting my body to turn to stone, 'When I say we are all going, it means exactly that, do you hear me young lady, you included?', she bawled out at me.

We hadn't been there for more than a couple of years when my father and mother were involved in a head on collision with a big lorry. They both survived the accident but, alas, my father died six days later from injuries received. My mother on the other hand had received another blow to the head, which in the coming years was to prove to be her down fall. That was eight years ago.

To see mother and I out we were almost identical in appearance .....you might even say like twins. She was a very beautiful black haired attractive woman but, alas, we didn't share much in common. Over the past eight years since the accident, I've witnessed a comparatively calm and sweet tempered woman turn into a sour, hideous monster. One minute she would be all smiles and happy- go- lucky, then, at the blink of an eye, her whole mood would change into something I can only describe as being hideous; It was just as though her whole being, had been possessed. Her black hair would stand up all bedraggled and her eyes would stare at you like a lifeless doll, then she would start hurling abuse at you, making the lives of my sisters and myself hell. But these tantrums never seemed to last long. It was only in the last few months of her life when they seemed to go on and on endlessly.

It was during this period of time in her life she brought a man home one night and introduced him as her boyfriend. My sisters and I had the shock of our lives, she was a very attractive woman, but her new boyfriend was anything but perfect. He always wore clothes that didn't suit him,he didn't like washing or shaving very often, in fact he was a right weirdo. He had the kind of eyes that seemed to transfix on you and you could feel his eyes undressing you, garment by garment he gave me the creeps!. When the subject of him was brought up in front of my mother, she would always defend him and a row would then start.

At this period in our lives we had few friends due to my mother's behaviour. Then a month ago my mother accused me of flirting with her boyfriend. This made me very angry and an almighty fight broke out between all parties, involving my two sisters and I, Mom and her boyfriend with the end result being my mother battering her new boyfriend half to death in a fit of rage and my sisters and I receiving bruises in the skirmish.

Her mood swings would change like the tide. Seeing what she had done she became hysterical and started crying out loud, eventually running out of the house and driving off in my sister's car. A few days later, her naked body was found floating in our local pool. Her boyfriend also died of his injuries in hospital later that week from the awful beating he had received".

As Lydia concluded her story, tears were streaming down her face.

The coroner's verdict was recorded on Catherine McGuire as suicide while the balance of her mind was disturbed.

Detective inspector Ben Roberts, who had worked on the Catherine Mc Guire suicide case, was enjoying some well earned leave with his family and friends on a beautiful island in the Bahamas. Having a mania for walking, one day while strolling leisurely along the beach, he got into conversation with another fellow Englishman also enjoying the delights of this enchanting island. The tone of the conversation swung around to the jobs they both did. His new found friend was a Doctor.... Andrew Meloa. Over the next few days meeting as they did, during their walks along the golden sands, they had many discussions on various topics, during one such conversation the name Catherine McGuire was mentioned.

Hearing the name made the doctor stop dead in his tracks, "Did you say Catherine Mc Guire?" he asked.

" Yes," answered Ben Roberts. " A very attractive black-haired beauty who, I'm sorry to say, is now deceased. She battered her boyfriend half to death, ran screaming out of her home and committed suicide. Her naked body was found three days later floating in a local pool".

Andrew Meloa seemed very alarmed at the tone of the story he had just been told. "I find this very hard to believe-I've known Catherine McGuire a great number of years, since we were at school together. You couldn't have found a more sweet- natured girl anywhere, and as for murder and suicide, that is right out of character. She was married to a very close friend of mine Ralph McGuire. They had three daughters, Lydia, Esther and Catherine. On my father's retirement I took over his practice and I was their family doctor. We've spent many happy hours, my wife and I, at parties and barbecues given by them. It was always a pleasure talking to Catherine as she was a good listener and conversationalist. Nothing was ever too much trouble if you had the time you could sit and talk to her all day.

On the other hand", the whole tone of his voice changed, "there was their eldest daughter Lydia. She was a problem child always getting into scraps and mischief. If there was a black sheep in any family, she was it. One incident I recall to mind, when she was at college she had a small cherub tattooed on her left hip, just small enough to be hidden by her bikini. When her mother saw it she went absolutely berserk. This caused a lot of friction in the family I can tell you. Mrs McGuire / Catherine was forever breaking up fights between her and her sister Esther. Honestly, that young madam has a lot to answer for in this whole sad affair".

As Ben listened to his new friend's explanations he began to get more and more disillusioned with the out -come of the case.

" Doctor, you say Lydia Mc Guire had a tattoo of a small cherub on her left hip.?"

"That's quite correct", answered Doctor Meloa.

"Because the body that was in our mortuary also has had a small cherub tattoo on the left hip".

"Are you sure you have the right body?" inquired the doctor. "Because when a person has a split personality they can easily take on an others identity. If you intend pursuing this case any further, I would tread very carefully if I were you. I've known cases in the past where you could be talking to a person with this condition thinking they're normal one minute, then, in the batting of an eye, you're facing an uncontrollable monster.

On his return home from his vacation. Ben immediately opened up the case files on Catherine McGuire and to his horror, the photographs taken of the nude victim clearly showed a small cherub tattoo on her left hip. " If this tattoo distinguishes the difference between mother and daughter, then the mother must still be alive". Thinking back now, during her evidence in the courtroom relating to her mother's suicide, Lydia wore dark glasses hiding some bruises to her face caused by a fracas with her late mother. Or was it the other way round.? These questions kept bombarding Ben's mind. "How could we have got the case wrong, or was it more than just a suicide?. There's only one way to find out that's go and pay the McGuire girls a visit at their factory on the other side of town".

Arriving next day at the factory, he and a female colleague were shown into a very big, lavishly- furnished office. Sitting behind a desk was Lydia Mc Guire. Her face and posture held both detectives spellbound -it was like looking at a replica of the photographs on their file of Catherine McGuire.

They introduced themselves and gave their reasons for being there. "During the last few days new evidence has been passed to us concerning a small cherub tattoo. We would like to clear up any loose ends in this sad tragedy and close the case for good". Ben began by telling Lydia McGuire his meeting with Doctor Meloa and their conversations concerning the McGuire family. Lydia seemed to be lost in space as she listened to the detective inspector outlining his story and the reason to question her more fully.

Lydia smiled as he ended his account of the new evidence

they had received, pushing her well formed figure into the back of the chair she then began telling the two detectives her side of the story.

"As you can see by your time spent with our good doctor and the stories he has told you about me, they are all true I won't deny a thing. I wasn't as you might say mommy's little angel, in fact just the opposite. You can see by those photographs in your case file that my mother and I were identical in looks, body, and posture but that is the only similarity. We were as different in our temperaments as chalk and cheese. My mother Catherine McGuire was a perfect lady, the way she walked and talked, her composure and posture-everything fitted into place, clothes, everything, had to match up, not even a hair out of place.

Everything that is until the day I arrived on the scene, I might have inherited her genes for looks and beauty but in temperament I was more like my Dad. Quite the opposite you might say as the family regarded me as a mud lark rather than a little angel. Growing up into my teen years it was a full time job trying to keep me clean and tidy. After a rain storm, I used to take great delight in jumping in all the deep muddy puddles I could find; this didn't impress my mother one little bit."

'One childhood memory I recall to mind still brings a smile to my face, I must have been about ten at the time, it happened many miles away on the east coast of England during the early part of my life. Having a large house in the country, as my parents had lots of money. We had a pet labrador dog called Jasper. Taking him for walks over the fields by our home, those are memories I will cherish until the end of my days. There was a large pond in the middle of this one field- that used to fascinate me it was filled with frogs, newts, fish, birds, and wild flowers of every description. Throwing stones and skimming them across the water was a hobby of mine counting each splash the stones made. This one particular day I was walking too close to the water's edge, when Jasper caught me off guard and sent me tumbling into the muddy, slimy water. Walking back home soaking wet, every time I stepped forward my shoes would squeak with the water trapped inside them. My mother was talking to my younger sister Esther, aged nine, in our kitchen that overlooked our back lawn, as I dragged my muddy water logged-body across it. "Esther tell me I'm dreaming or having a nightmare ! Is that thing walking over our lawn covered in mud and slime my eldest daughter?."

Esther replied, "Yes mom it is" .

"She came charging out of the house like a bull elephant grabbing me by my shoulder and growling at me, "Cant you ever keep clean?". She literally ripped the clothes off my body. "You're not coming into my house with those muddy things on", she said," not on your life".

Taking the garden hose she then proceeded to hose down my naked body, with me screaming my head off, that water was stone cold. She then yelled out an order to Esther.

"Get me a big towel from the bathroom at once do you hear me"!.

Recalling this particular incident she began laughing to herself. " I admit this myself, I was no angel. Esther on the other hand was a little angel, my mother's pride and joy she couldn't do a thing wrong in my mother's eyes. She was one year younger than me. My dad loved is fishing but to pacify our mother he had to take Esther and me with him as a added bonus this he didn't like.

" This one particular day, I recall it vividly". she began smiling to herself. " He had gotten up early and dug some worms up in the garden to catch some fish. Esther and I sat on the pool's bank watching him bored out of our brains. I then began teasing Esther with one of the worms out of dads bait tin she responded to my teasing by pushing me. We both started fighting on the bank, finally winding up in the pool with an almighty splash.

Dad was furious, "you wait until your mother sees the state of you two, she'll go barmy," came his reply.

One night while sitting on our settee, mother came and sat down next to me, and began talking.

"Why can't you be like Esther, a good girl, and keep out of

trouble?. I'm wasting no more time smacking you with my hands".

" I thought to myself at the time, now isn't that considerate and kind.? No more hidings. She then finished her sentence."

"I'm going to start to belt you with that clothes brush instead young lady, if you don't start and behave".

Looking shocked I replied," yes Mom".

"Lydia, you're now a teenager- you will soon be a young women, then start college. What profession at college would you like to train for?."

Immediately I responded, "a motor mechanic," Tinkering about and repairing old engines is a favourite pastime of mine.

" Over my dead body! You can forget that daft idea," she shouted out aloud. "No daughter of mine is going to grovel in filthy oil and grease, I'll enrol you in something I find suitable".

" Choosing my own subject is my choice," I answered her back.

" You will do as I say young lady and that is final" .

"For my insolence I then spent the next four years at college learning about pharmacy and chemistry. As regards to the tattoo you mentioned, it's a little cherub. I had it done at college- you can imagine what my mother said about that. My explanation was a friend had been killed in a car accident and the only visible proof of identity was a small tattoo so all the members of our particular circle of college friends all had one done in exactly the same place to prove our identities. I was now as big as my mother and a spanking was well out of the question so she let it go at that."

AII the while she was talking Ben kept thinking to himself, the mother is a very good impersonator, or Lydia is the real thing but I still have an ace up my sleeve, the cherub tattoo. Ben then began bombarding her with questions hoping she would slip up and reveal her true identity. It was like listening to someone reading from a script his barrage of questions were met with truthful answers.

She started reminiscing again. " Twelve years ago the whole family moved to the north east of England and we have been here ever since. My father started up these factories I 'm pleased to say, they have been a good investment. At the death of my father, my mother wanted nothing at all to do with the running of them, so my two sisters and I picked up the gauntlet and took on the challenge and ran the factories. My job being production and maintenance manager. Esther, and Catherine, marketing and sales, we sell machine components all over the world.

Now let's get back to the question of this cherub tattoo that I presume is the reason for your visit here".

The way that last remark came out of the blue caught Ben completely by surprise.

She continued,"If your lady assistant would like to follow me into the ladies room we can soon get this misunderstanding cleared up".

It was the first time since arriving and sitting in Lydia's office Ben felt confident. 'Now I've got you', Ben thought to himself, 'Try and talk yourself out of this one'.

Both ladies emerged a few minutes later.

"There is definitely a small cherub tattoo on her left hip" the police woman told her boss.

Ben looked puzzled and mystified, at her last remark. That's impossible he thought to himself

Lydia sat with her backside perched on the side of the desk as she faced the two detectives, "Let me just clarify and make clear a few minor points if I may; I can see by your faces you're both looking confused and puzzled. During my late mother's illness one day she said to me, 'when you showed me your little cherub tattoo and explained the reason for having it done, I couldn't believe it at the time thinking it was another one of your stupid excuses, but giving the matter a lot of thought it really does make sense . That accident involving me and your father, what would have happened if we had been that badly burned it would have been impossible to identify us?."

This statement she made took me completely by surprise. After making so much fuss and commotion about the one I had done. She persuaded me to take her to the shop to get a little cherub, tattooed on her left hip the same as mine. The only difference being if you look carefully in the middle of the cherub on mine there's a tiny, 'L' for Lydia, on my mothers its a tiny 'C' for Catherine. I hope my answers to your questions have proved to be satisfactory.

Catherine McGuire, my mother, whom I loved and worshipped she was a very beautiful and talented woman. I'm just a mere replica. But I say this now to you in all honesty, I've lived my life to the full and wouldn't change it for the world. Like all parents my mother had my life planned out for me, whom I should marry and the kind of friends I should have. Until one day I threw a spanner in the works and told her I was pregnant. A college friend of mine had been commuting across the country every weekend to see me. We have been happily married now these past six years having a little boy whom I love to bits and a husband I adore".

The inspector nodded his head as he got up off his chair and walked to the door followed in hot pursuit by his female colleague. Turning to face Lydia he spoke, "The case file on Catherine McGuire I'm glad to say is now finally closed "

Esther entered her sisters office a few minutes later, "What did they want'?, she inquired.

Lydia began, "Our old friend Doctor Andrew Meloa had told the inspector about my cherub tattoo".

"Doctor Meloa has never liked you since you loosed his tyres down when you were young". Esther was giggling to herself as she spoke, she was not unlike her sister in looks and appearance, the only difference being she had blonde hair.

Sitting on the corner of the desk facing Lydia, she was now laughing hysterically as she reminded Lydia of her past escapades she could hardly get the words out.

" That... day..... Mom.... tanned.... your... backside.... with.... a clothes brush... for... messing.... with... the... doctors.... car, every... whack,... was... followed... by.. a high.. pitched... scream. I've never laughed so much in my whole life. Its a wonder your bum isn't flat from the hidings you have received in the past for playing up. "This last remark sent the quivers down her body making her rock with laughter.

Lydia looked at her sister laughing at her expense, picking up a plastic ruler off her desk and smacking it across her hand she stood up and faced Esther .

"So you think me screaming out in pain was funny do you"?,

"I think it was hilarious, I can count my good hidings on one hand, I would need twenty hands to count yours", Esther replied to her sister, trying to keep a straight face.

"What's the old saying sister dear, he who laughs least, laughs last, lets see if I can carve my initials on your well rounded rump with this ruler, shall we". came Lydia's sarcastic reply.

"You wouldn't dare", protested Esther

"Just you watch me", answered Lydia and lunged at her sister.

THE END

Demidrogs

Night time on a quiet and peaceful little island in the Caribbean, sea spray lapping at the rocks as the sea pushes its way up the sandy beach, palm trees and jungle foliage growing in profusion along the waters edge. On this hot summers evening the air is alive with merriment, fires have been lit, and decorations adorned the little huts along the shore line. As the villagers on this remote island sing and dance the night away to celebrate with an exceptional feast, the birth of a son born to their chief's wife. In the sea around its shores as moonbeams make pretty patterns on the waters surface. Marine life teeming with abundance as silver flashes in the water indicate shoals of fish jumping and darting about, as though a huge predator had driven the smaller fish into the shallows making them leap out of the water to escape. Sea birds were also enjoying this rare sight by diving into the sea to catch a tasty morsel. Fish of all shapes and sizes were jumping out of the sea and into the air, some to catch small fry, others the fear of being eaten. This marine aerobatics display had bought many of the curious islanders onto the beach to watch in wonder at this once in a lifetime spectacle. Some wading waist deep into the water to keep cool on this very hot summers night to watch and enjoy the spectacular water aquatics. An ear piercing, high pitched whistle made the air vibrate all around as it travelled over the air waves forcing the revellers to clap their hands over their ears to keep out the agonising sound. Many of the villagers were scanning the waters of the ocean with their eyes trying to find out what was causing this mysterious high pitched sound.

A terrifying scream suddenly rings out, as a man is dragged under the waves, then another, and another, and yet another. Panic has now sent everyone wading back to the shore all floundering and falling flat on their faces as they too are systematically dragged back into the sea. People standing on the sandy beach are helpless and horrified as though in a state of shock at what is going on in front of their very eyes, watching friends and relations suddenly disappearing under the waves. Villagers going to the aid of loved ones are being caught up in this carnage and experiencing the same fate as they too are being attacked and dragged under the water. Suddenly emerging from the sea like a huge brown blanket of mud and racing up the beach at an alarming rate, like a swarm of hungry locusts ready to devour a field of grain. Hundreds of centipede like creatures their teeth gnashing together make short work of what is left of the remaining villagers, who tried in vain to stave off their attackers but are quickly subdued by sheer weight of numbers. As the screams and cries die away helpless bodies lie paralysed everywhere as ferocious jaws begin ripping the flesh away devouring every warm blooded living thing in sight .

Two weeks later news had reached the mainland of this terrible catastrophe, sent in by a patrol vessel keeping the sea lanes safe in the area. Immediately the research ship 'Neptune' was dispatched post haste to the area to investigate this strange phenomena. Dropping anchor a mile off shore its motor launches were lowered into the sea. Members of the crew looked bewildered at the island shore line clambering up the beach for the first time rifles at the ready, fingers twitching nervously on the triggers. Their eyes were paralysed with fear at the sight that lay ahead of them. All what was left of the nine hundred and fifty islanders were heaps of skeletons scattered everywhere not a bit of flesh has been left on the bones as they lay bleaching in the midday sun. No one had survived the attack, young and old alike even pets had all suffered the same fate all had been slaughtered in this blood thirsty carnage.

A strange looking sea creature was discovered, as they began the harrowing task of removing the skeletons of the villagers for burial as they searched among the debris. To the naked eye it resembled a large centipede, it was dark brown in colour with fifty legs each side of its long narrow body,and it was approximately four feet long. On its head protruding upwards were two pointed horns. It's broad flat mouth was full of very sharp razor like teeth.

News of the amazing discovery was immediately radioed back to the mainland base laboratory, together with photographs sent over the telex for research and investigation to find out what kind of creature it was and how it could be tackled. No records or information of any description regarding this strange looking insect like creature could be found. It was a complete new strain. Its carcass was cut and dissected to try and find out its origin, scientists were flown in from various parts of the world to give advice on their findings but all drew a blank. This mysterious sea creature had them all baffled, working day and night carrying out experiments the laboratory technicians were trying different combinations to try and find out how this multi-legged creature functioned.

Meanwhile a thousand miles away on one of the Caribbean's larger islands a passenger steamer was unloading its passengers onto a wooden jetty jutting out into the sea. Most of them plantation workers returning home from work on neighbouring islands, the others tourists out for the day sight seeing. All of them idly talking among themselves as they walked along the dimly lit jetty leading to a small coastal town. A strange high pitched whistle began filling the air waves causing havoc as the ferry passengers tried in vain to cover their ears to keep out the agonising sound. What lay in front of them on the jetty in the evenings half light was even more confusing, it looked as though some one had tipped tons of brown soil blocking their path. Getting ever nearer to this strange sight, they were suddenly confronted by a thousand eyes staring at them. As if someone had suddenly switched on the fairy lights of a giant Christmas tree. Hundreds of gleaming vicious gnashing teeth were reflected in the moonlight, sending the ferry passenger racing headlong back along the jetty in terror tumbling over one another in their panic to try and reboard the ferry. But alas they were to late it had already cast off and was sailing away in the distance. They were caught like rats in a trap screams and squeals were of no avail as this large pack of insect like creatures started ripping the flesh from their bodies. All that was left of the one hundred and twenty passengers from the ferry in the dim light of dawn where piles of bones on the end of the jetty. Some of them lucky enough to escape by jumping into the sea all suffered a similar fate, there were no survivors.

Attacks of this magnitude were becoming an every day occurrence as more and more people fell victim to this strange phenomena. Lonely desert island outposts once places of tranquil beauty places to relax and forget life's worries were now becoming prime targets as the precidented attacks continued. A group of children happily playing and swimming in the mouth of a river estuary on a hot summers evening had suddenly disappeared without trace.

Investigations being carried out by inspectors from neighbouring communities concurred that all attacks had been carried out at night, as if the perpetrators were frightened of direct sunlight. It was like an epidemic out of all proportion sweeping through the Caribbean as terrified islanders flocked to the mainland for safety.

Scientists working on this strange project had been told of a man who lived alone on a small peninsular on the main land. Reports stated he was a retired ocean scientist and had made oceanography his life's work studying the mysteries of the sea and its strange phenomena, especially around the Caribbean area of the world. The cottage in which he resided backed into a large collection of subterranean caves and caverns that went down deep into the bowels of the earth.

Immediately a team was dispatched post haste comprising of a man and a woman, to question the old man on the knowledge they had, and maybe get some answers and find a solution to their problems.

Approaching the old mans residence was like nothing they had ever seen on this earth before. It was a strange experience in itself. Whale bones formed a large entrance covered in creeping grape vines that had twisted and entwined around the bones giving of a dashing array of colour. Brightly coloured sea shells of every size and shape completely covered the large two bed-roomed cottage leaded windows sparkled in the suns rays, making the sight even more spectacular. Large areas of ground had been cultivated to provide vegetables thus making him self sufficient. Chickens and ducks roamed around at will, and two white goats occupied a small enclosure providing the owner with all the milk he wanted and to top it all, two black and white collie dogs acted as guard dogs, whose continual barking had made the old man emerge from his cottage.

After all the introductions had been made the team were invited inside by their host for some refreshments A tall thin grey haired old man with a small goatee type beard who spoke perfect English gave them a guided tour of his domain. His smartness in dress suggested a regimental up bringing. Inside the cottage it was like being in Alladins cave being spotlessly clean with furniture carved from old drift wood, porcelain ornaments decorated its window sills and tribal masks and human skulls hung on the walls.

A huge desk carved in wood stood in the middle of the main room taking preference over everything else, its top covered in papers and old manuscripts. Two bedrooms had been strategically placed on the side of the dwelling to keep out the midday sun. After gulping down a nice refreshing cool drink given to them by their host. They began explaining their mission to the old man by showing him photographs of their mysterious quarry. Both scientists, Brendan Smythe, and Laura Jackson, were then invited to follow him down into the tunnels leading to the subterranean caverns.

Going down those spooky tunnels in near pitch black darkness, the only light being from a bunch of oil filled rags on the end of a stick was enough to put the fear of God in to anybody. Everywhere in amongst the numerous hanging cobwebs the walls were decorated with coloured pictures, of trees, animals, birds, and flowers, depicting a bygone age. Tunnels in the caverns carved out by time itself seemed to be long dark and endless, finally opening out at last into a huge gallery filled with stalactites and stalagmites.

Suddenly they were confronted by a drawing on a wall in

front of them reminding them of their mission. a number of coloured pictures had been drawn of their mysterious sea creature. When questioned about this particular painting the old man replied.

"It has taken me countless years of study and also my father before me. Gathering information from various sources, drawings and writings on the walls, between us over the years we have managed to piece together its brief history. A name given to it by the people who inhabited these caves hundreds of years ago, was, Demidrog, or the sea creatures from hell.

His answers to their questions were beginning to send cold shivers of fright right down to the toes of the research team as he continued his story. ...."Demidrog as you can see by the paintings on the walls it's similar to an oversized centipede with three exceptions, one being a mouthful of razor sharp teeth, the other, two long thin horns which can deliver a killer sting, its venom killing in seconds, and the third, being a piercing high pitched whistle that can burst your eardrums and render you helpless. In the lower levels of these caves skeletons of men women and children have been found but also fossilised remains of their attackers, Demidrogs. Intensive studies made by me over the years of this creature have made one thing very clear, the people who inhabited these caves were the only people left alive in this region A prophecy written by one of the late inhabitants of these caves has been translated by my father and I to read.

One day an eruption out of all proportion on the oceans floor would again awaken the Demidrogs from their slumber and they would return and once again reign havoc over the earth.

During their last appearance in this region where they literally gobbled up every warm blooded creature in sight wiping out man kind as we now it. Writings on the walls although in strange hieroglyphics, over the years with much patience I have been able to translate. A huge egg laying Queen rules and controls the colony of Demidrogs the same as a Queen bee in a hive.Their basic staple diet is phantom and seaweed. When a disturbance down in the depths on the oceans floor caused by a major volcanic eruption or earthquake limits her food chain. This results in her laying eggs by the million who hatch out into blood thirsty carnivores. Who come up from the depths of the ocean to the surface and devour a region of warm blooded mammals like locusts ravaging a field of grain. Bright light and the sun's rays dries out the moisture content in their bodies resulting in death. That is why the attacks you have explained to me only happen at night.

Research has provided the last known outbreak of this kind happened when an underground volcano erupted in the Atlantic, hundreds of years ago, followed by volcanic ash blotting out the suns rays and cooling the earths surface down which I can only assume wiped them all out. Over the years the human race have hunted certain animals to extinction now if the Demidrogs are not stopped they will do the same to you.

After returning to the mainland laboratory with their fact finding mission complete,Brendan Smythe, and Laura Jackson, made out their respective reports for their superiors. Where on top scientists were called in, to ponder over the old man's theories, and prophecy's, concerning this mysterious sea creature. Most of them were in agreement as the answers were straight forward and simple. Today's technology differed greatly from hundreds of years ago, with modern day techniques it would be an easy task to track down these perpetrators and destroy them in their thousands.

Even as they worked out a solution in their laboratories, every day more reports were coming in of bodies found stripped right down to the bone on remote islands and whole communities wiped out. the main areas of attack being in the Caribbean part of the world.

So once again the research ship 'Neptune' was ordered to sea. this time with the idea of capturing one alive so that experiments could be carried out to find out more about these centipede like sea creatures. Sailing at full speed the 'Neptune' made its way to the Caribbean to endeavour to capture a Demidrog alive.

*   *   *   *   *

Two small luxury cruisers doing a sight seeing trip of the Caribbean's many islands, had moored in a beautiful secluded cove, both passengers and crew enjoying the delights which these enchanted islands bring. All who were aboard the two vessels had waded ashore then began collecting drift wood for a fire to use as a barbecue to cook some meat and fish on, the idea being to wine, dine and dance the night away. An elderly man was the only passenger left aboard on the two cruisers, he had been complaining of head aches and stomach pains, and had decided to call it a day and have an early night. His last glimpse of his relations and friends before retiring saw them dancing and singing on the beach just as the sun was setting below the horizon. As the singing dancing and frivolities continued on into the early hours of the morning, a young man snatches a swimming bra off a young woman and goes racing into the sea with it. With the young woman in hot pursuit, both of them diving under the waves as their friends their faces beaming with laughter their watchful eyes waiting for them to re-emerge.

Minutes began ticking away but there no sign of either person breaking the surface. So two more young men dived in to try and find out what had happened to their friends. Then two more,and then two girls joined in the search. All splashing about in the water their eyes scouring the bottom gulping in air in order to dive deeper under the water. As they searched among the seaweed and coral, they too became victims disappearing into the depths never to be seen again. Their friends and colleagues now paddling waist deep in water to try and find the answer to their friends disappearance. Found themselves now under attack and being dragged under the waves by an unknown assailant. Panic had reached fever pitch as the remainder looked at the calm clear water and were faced with the harsh reality that their friends had gone, never again to return. Suddenly the water began to bubble and boil around the shore line as brown muti-legged creatures came racing out of the sea scouring the beach for prey. What was left of the surviving men and women were sent tumbling over one another trying to escape. No one survived the devastating attack on the beach that night. In the morning the tell tale sign of bones bleached by the morning sun was all that was left of the beach party.

Fatigue had caused the old man to sleep well into the morning and on awakening his first thought was a nice refreshing cup of coffee. Then a walk around the deck to blow the cobwebs away. Taking very ungainly steps he began inching his way along the safety rail as his eyes now dim with age searched the beach line for his friends and relations. But there was no one to be seen. The island cove was completely deserted. In his desperation he made his way to the wheel house and there began blowing the cruisers horn to try and attract someone's attention ashore, but no one answered, he was completely alone. He began fumbling with the radio to try and summon help, his eye sight began playing tricks on him as he turned and twisted the various dials on the radio.

Six days later on a peaceful Sunday evening as the congregation of island villagers were attending evening prayer, at a small coastal town church, sounds of their hymn singing floated gently over the oceans waves. On a shingle beach only yards away, seven new arrivals to the island where all eager to try out their new fishing tackle, casting out their different baits into the sea to try and tice the fish to bite. Suddenly a shout goes up from one of them as his rod bends and bows taking the strain of his catch, then another, and another, until all seven were struggling with their rods. All hoping to out do his opponent by playing and landing a specimen fish. One of the seven anglers playing his fish to try and tire it out, was now faced with a new dilemma as his fishing line suddenly goes racing off his reel at an alarming rate.

"Look sharks" one frantically calls out as he points out fins protruding above the waters surface,"There must be hundreds of them".

Just as the sun was having its final fling for the day before disappearing below the horizon leaving its tell tale golden streaks across the ocean's surface. Each of the seven fishermen were now experiencing the same problem as their friend, as though big preditors had gobbled up their catch. Water was sent cascading up into the air, and huge waves crashing against the shore line as the sharks went on a feeding frenzy fighting amongst each other for the tasty morsels. Lines on most of the fishermens reels had now broken being caused by the heavy weights arriving in the waters.

Using all the strength in is body he could muster one remaining fisherman with the only unbroken line slowly begins winding in his reel, bringing his prize catch to the shore. Eager hands reaching out to help him get it onto the beach. He had successfully landed a small shark about six feet in length. In it's mouth a strange looking brown object which resembled a very large Rag worm which had taken anglers bait. Bending down to examine it more closely all of them began scratching their heads. Whatever can it be? Was this the reason for the shark invasion. Even as they chatted amongst themselves the water was beginning to calm down as the big predators were now returning to the deeper parts of the ocean after filling their bellies.

A bizarre sight opened the eyes of one early morning tourist has he lazily walked along the beach in the dawns hot sun. Bodies of four large sharks were slowly being tossed to and fro by the tide and surrounding them like a blanket of brown foam on the oceans surface, were countless brown legs heads and bodies that had been bitten off by their attackers.

*   *   *   *   *

Beautiful clear blue skies and the oceans surface as flat as a board welcomed, the 'Neptune', as it reached it's planned destination. Specially adapted under-water marine craft had been lowered into the depths to search the ocean floor for their quarry. Brendan Smythe, and Laura Jackson, had been given the harrowing task of capturing a Demidrog alive. Using modern day technology their echo sounders were bouncing off anything large in the area, from shoals of fish to whales and sharks, all sightings being recorded and monitored by their computers.

Huge search lights on their bathyscaphe were crisscrossing as they patiently scoured the sea bed. Suddenly Laura Jackson let out a scream and pointing.

"Look, in front of us"

For captured in the beams of their search lights were three Demidrogs feeding on young shoots on a huge clump of sea weed. They seemed paralysed by the strong bright light, having the same effect as getting a rabbit in your headlight beam on a road. Nets were quickly brought into operation and the three caught. Then quickly hauled to the surface and put in large water tanks aboard the research ship 'Neptune'.

Excited news of the capture was quickly radioed back to base, the message also included a line which read....... 'One of the Demidrogs is twice as big as the rest and nearly ten feet in length' with scales down it's back!

A message was relayed back instantly.

"This could be a Queen, return immediately back to base without any delay".

As the scientists aboard the research ship studied their new found specimens before weighing anchor. No one noticed a sudden movement in the anchor chain as hundreds of Demidrogs began climbing up it. Agonising high pitched whistles began filling the air waves making the crew cry out in agony as their eardrums began to burst.

They were now faced with a new frightening dilemma as the Demidrogs began clambering aboard in their hundreds. If it had been an old wooden sailing ship it would have been no contest, but with modern day technology and weapons, the ships metal doors, the crew were able to turn the tables and contain them by closing the doors and trapping them inside. News of the invasion was immediately sent to their mainland base telling them of their success in defending their ship against attack and capturing even more Demidrogs.

Everyone at the base was jubilant at the 'Neptune's' news. A successful mission was completed and now returning with even more live specimens made the scientists jump with joy. Now, in the space of a few more days the 'Neptune' would return to port and they could carry out their experiments.

Weather conditions were also in their favour as the research ship 'Neptune' sailed back to her home port through calm blue waters. Members of the crew were still complaining of the ever increasing volume of high pitched whistles, that was making then go deaf.

Waiting with anticipation for the research ships return to port to deliver its valuable cargo. Scientists were busy getting their equipment ready to carry out experiments on these strange sea creatures. But the days dragged into weeks then months. Intensive searches were carried out with aircraft and warships covering the whole area but the 'Neptune' had just completely disappeared without trace. This came as a body blow to the organisers. What had gone wrong the last message received from the 'Neptune' had said.

'Returning back to base with cargo as ordered,visibility excellent, sea, dead calm'.

Was this yet another casualty of the mysterious Bermuda triangle? Had it claimed another unsuspecting victim? Had the black hole sucked down another helpless ship?. One explanation put forward by one of the scientists was that, Wasps and Bees, rely on their Queens to lay eggs to multiply and would defend her to the death, was this the case with the Demidrogs?. What if our men had captured the Queen and the attack on the boat was an attempt to release her?. We shall never know for the answer lies out there, at the bottom of the sea. No more attacks or sightings were ever reported the whole Demidrog phenomena had just fizzled out.

THE END

Echoes from the Grave

A warm summer Sunday afternoon with clear blue skies and a light breeze fanning the air just enough to make you sit down and relax, watching with interest as a large bumble bee struggles with his legs to open the large petals on one of the flowers in my back garden . The sweet smell of lavender tantalising my nostrils with its perfume, as I sat on my garden swing and as it lazily rocked me backwards and forwards, backwards and forwards. What could be more peaceful on this glorious sunny afternoon.?

A female voice shouting down the garden shatters the silence and my thoughts.

"Fred..... telephone ".

Getting off my swing and cursing with every step I took, now who the hell can this be, and how dare they break the peace and solitude of my Sunday afternoon rest. Picking up the telephone,

"Hello Fred Dimmock speaking".

A voice on the other end answered, "Fred its me George Sanderson", and they were only words I got out of the whole conversation. I couldn't get a word in edgewise he kept on, and on, and on, until he eventually rang off leaving me standing there speechless holding the telephone.

My wife Mary broke the silence. "who was that Fred"?.

Looking at her in disbelief I replied, "that was George Sanderson he wants to come and see me next Saturday afternoon, he sounded very worried and agitated ".

"When was the last time you saw George,?".....Mary enquired

"It has got to be at least fifteen years if its a day, do you remember we both attended his wife,: Joan's funeral?". looking at his wife puzzled, "remember the old saying Mary, a friend in need is a friend indeed. Lets find out what he wants".

Mary smiled as she spoke to her husband , her long grey hair hanging over her spectacles as she worked on a patchwork quilt. "How old would George Sanderson be now"?".

Fred scratched his head, "George is a year older than me making him... sixty seven".

Saturday afternoon I was like a cat on hot bricks, looking out of our downstairs lounge window every few minutes waiting for my old friend to arrive, when suddenly a brand new car pulled up outside our house. This took me completely by surprise, remembering the last time I saw him he hadn't got two pennies to rub together. Watching him walk up our garden path I had to admire him. His tall slim figure, tailor made suit, a tan, the envy of everyone, and a full head of thick grey hair combed neatly to one side. Glancing into our lounge mirror I mumbled to myself, "why has he got so much hair, and me, nothing!", stroking my bald head. After a rapturous reunion and handshakes all around he began telling me the reason for his unscheduled visit...... And to this very day I wish he hadn't.. Mary and myself got engrossed in his story and were spellbound as he outlined his tale of woe to us.

"Last year a cousin of mine sent me a book of unsolved crime stories. After flitting through the pages, a story caught my eye and imagination. It was about a man called Job Measham who supposedly murdered three nine year old school girls. After reading it. I couldn't get the story out of my mind the whole sad saga, held me like a magnet and I kept reading the story over, and over again looking at his pathetic little face on a photograph on one of the pages. The bodies of the three children were never found and he was convicted on purely circumstantial evidence, and finally sentenced to a minimum of fifteen years. His plea being , that he was innocent. I felt sorry for him. After serving ten years of his sentence they found him hanging in is cell one morning, a suicide note left by him told its own tragic story. Still demanding there had been a miscarriage of justice and that he was innocent.

Whether or not his story had got to me I shall never know because every time I closed my eyes his face was haunting me. Night and day always saying the same thing over and over again,

'I'm innocent ,I'm innocent, will some one help me?',

'You know Fred, I have never experienced a sensation like it before in my whole life and that's the honest truth. If I wasn't a rational person I would swear I was going out of my mind. I'm frightened to go to sleep at night ; his face is always there staring at me and haunting me.

According to the story in the book Job committed suicide two years ago allegedly from being bullied and tormented in prison by his fellow inmates. They found him hanging in his cell one morning after having served ten years of his fifteen year sentence. His demise led to a journalist writing this story. All the evidence that had been collected against him was circumstantial. He was seen chasing after the three youngsters down a pathway in a place called Copthorn Woods after a passer-by had seen the children throwing stones at his window. They found one of the children's' handkerchiefs in his possession. He claimed one of the children had dropped it and he had picked it up. Then after an intensive search of the woods and neighbouring woodlands no sign was ever found of the three girls' bodies. So Job Measham became their number one suspect. Then in the remains of a bonfire that had been lit in his garden, and although the ashes had been scattered to the four winds, traces of a dress were found. The theory then being at the time that he had murdered the three little girls and burnt their bodies on the bonfire. In a statement made by him he claimed he had burned some of his late mother's clothes on the bonfire in his garden. This sounded feasible enough except for one article of attire that clinched his fate. One of the little girls shoes were found in the undergrowth by his back gate. When questioned about this, he didn't have an answer.

All through his trial he repeated over and over again,' you have got it wrong', you have the wrong man I am innocent'.

"Fred I can't see me ever having a good night's sleep again until I have been to Copthorm woods and investigated the crime for myself, what do you say do you fancy a trip in the fresh air.?"

Looking at him I just couldn't believe what I had just heard, thinking for a minute about his hair brained scheme, then before I could give him an answer, Mary butted into the conversation.

"Why not," she said, "its a marvellous idea that will give me chance to catch up on my needle and craft work".

Smiling at my wife I said to him, "Well that's been decided, when do we start?".

"Fred you might as well know," smiling all over his face as he spoke, I've been told on good authority there is a big lake in Copthorn woods and it is full of big carp, so we can take our fishing tackle with us and do a bit of fishing during our search........shall we say.... next Saturday the 11th July?. Accommodation can be arranged and I will telephone you with all the details. Copthorn village, it's on the map. About fifty miles from here.

"That will suit me fine George, do you mind If I bring another friend along he is also a fisherman, my neighbour Sam?".

"No" replied George, "the more the merrier"

*   *   *   *   *

"It looks as though we could be in for a spell of nice weather the reports look very favourable", commented Sam as we made our way down the winding country lanes in my old car, banging, and bumping, as it bounced over the many pot holes in the road, eventually arriving at a sleepy little country village. Its sign read ....Welcome to Copthorn.

Directions George had given me simply said.

Turn left at the village pub ....THE SWAN..... go down a tree lined avenue, eventually opening up onto a large village green, on the right hand side a large white painted house that's called. The Meadows. That's our B&B for the week.

After booking in and exchanging greetings with my old friend it was decided amongst the three of us to take a walk and get the feel of our new surroundings. We were given strict instructions by our land lady, tea would be served at 6 o'clock on the dot.

Walking down the roads in that sleepy little village, George, Sam, and I, you could not visualise a barbarous act of murder ever taking place. Everything was so peaceful and quiet it was an idealistic little spot.

Approaching the village as we did from the main road we made our way back, until we came to a small side road with a sign saying 'Copthorn woods'. A small brook followed the road on the left hand side finally disappearing into a field. During our Saturday afternoon stroll, we passed a boarded up cottage which we assumed belonged to Job Measham. A pathway ran down the side of the cottage wall, eventually winding up in Copthorn woods. Taking on an adventure of this nature you don't realise the vast area that the woods actually cover. We started our painstaking search trying to piece together the last moments of the children's lives. We investigated the gate leading to Job's garden and we discovered a six foot high brick wall dividing the woods from the neighbouring fields and village. A small cultivated narrow field with green houses and garden produce growing in profusion ran parallel with the wall and at certain points along its length gardens from the village backed onto it.

Sitting down absolutely starving for our evening meal after a fruitless search in the woods, we were joined by two more guests both here on a fishing expedition, having introduced themselves and explaining the reason for their visit. One of our fellow guests Bert Jones, remarked to George,

"Do you realise how big Copthorn Woods actually are,?...I have been coming down here to fish the lake for years, you could hide an army in there. never mind three small children."

"Nevertheless" he replied "I shall never have a good night's sleep again if I at least don't try. Job Measham's face haunts me like a ghost from the past night and day. I can see that pleading look in his eyes, its a week out of my life and he has paid the supreme sacrifice by cutting short his, so the search must go on."

The determination in George's voice hit a nerve in Bert's body,

"Tell you what George. My mate Sid and I are here on a fishing trip, but we won't be fishing all the time so if you want two more volunteers we're your men".

At that an attractive woman in her early sixties entered the room. She had a cheeky grin across a very pretty face.

"My sister told me we had five handsome men staying here and now I"ve seen you all, it's certainly quite true. I am Martha and that's my sister June,"she said pointing at another very attractive female. "Tonight's menu, to start Mushroom soup, followed by homemade steak and kidney pie, new potatoes, beans, and peas, and then apple and blackberry pie with ice cream, are you all happy with that.?".

This was followed by a chorus from the guests of, " that will suit us all fine"

George stood up. He had a way with words especially when talking to attractive women, being an handsome man six feet tall and slim build he was a proper gentleman. "Let me introduce everyone this is Bert, Sid, Sam, Fred. And I'm George. Let me say this now, in all honesty, if your cooking tastes as good as you two look there will be no complaints from us".

All the while he was talking, Martha couldn't take her eyes off him. Her round pretty face, curly greying hair hanging down hiding a pair of brown spectacles digested every word that was spoken but there was warmth in her beautiful smile.

After sampling Martha and June's cooking, all five of them were fit to burst, but decided to go to Copthorn woods for a nice leisurely stroll to help digest their evening meal. At the same time they could try and pick up a few fishing tips from the anglers fishing around the lake. Finally rounding the night off by calling in for a pint at the village pub, then bed to resume their relentless search the following day.

It's surprising the way when you share a common interest how the conversation seems endless. Old George had the knack of telling soft little jokes that had them all in fits of laughter, and to top it all, when we finally arrived at the village pub, George's eye's lit up as he noticed an organ standing gathering dust in the corner. Shyly he asked the bar man, "who plays the organ?".

"You if you can". came back a witty reply "Right you're on. I'll make that organ talk, Fred give me a lift to pull it out a bit"

Getting himself comfortable on the stool George started playing a few classical pieces. It was a lovely warm summers night and there was a lot of people outside but when the music started they began to drift back in. Playing a repertoire of well known modern day songs and finally finishing off the night with a medley of the old favourite tunes like, Show me the way to go home Old George had them singing their little heads off.

Sunday morning after finishing off a well prepared breakfast, our gallant band began their quest to try and find enough evidence in Copthorn woods and the surrounding countryside to clear Job Meashams name. We searched along the length of the brook until it eventually ran into Copthorn lake, turning over every leaf and blade of grass climbing up trees and over boulders then the wood itself on and on looking into hollows made in trees, mounds of earth, for any tell tale sign... into..... Monday.... Tuesday..... Wednesday.... Thursday.... and finally Friday, stopping only to have our meals and a well deserved pint in the local pub. I have never known a week like it. Every morning being greeted by a big yellow sun shining out of a clear blue sky and the air warm and still with hardly a breeze. We couldn't have picked a more perfect week even if we had tried. On Thursday night enjoying a well earned pint, someone in the pub had told us to try a little wooded copse called, Copthorn Holloway bog. It was about half a mile away from the main wood. We thought we would try to see if it would change our luck. Our search was all in vain, climbing up trees, looking in the hollows, we even searched the bog with long sticks but nothing. George's face said it all, our efforts had been fruitless. The original search had proved nothing and our intensive search had also drawn a blank. Shaking every one by the hand and thanking them for giving up their valuable time and supporting him in his quest to try and clear an innocent man's name. We had done all that was humanly possible. We had tried but failed.

Sitting down on that final night for our evening meal the atmosphere was sombre. No one hardly making a sound. You could see that beaten look in George's eyes, Martha came in wearing a lovely off the shoulder, short sleeved summer dress, and after all the wolf whistles George plucked up the courage to ask her , 'what was the special occasion?'.

She replied, "my sister and I are going to a summer choral song concert at the village church hall, where they are hoping to raise enough funds to repair the church roof. On the programme the church choir will be singing some modern songs and also doing a medley from the shows".

"You know Martha that sounds absolutely fantastic. I could do with something to cheer me up, and what a way to end a perfect week,!..... well nearly perfect," giving a sigh, "there wouldn't by any chance be any spare tickets?, what do you say lads?" This last suggestion had bought some colour back into George's cheeks.

"If you're sure that's what you all want I can give the organiser Mary Peters a ring" Martha came back a few moments later, "there are six tickets left if you are still interested."

" We'll take them, I'm paying so no arguments, its a thank you for all the hard work you have put into my project. " George said smiling looking at his fellow guests.

They all looked at one another and smiling said, "yes"

" so that's settled then Martha."

"Its a lovely warm summers evening so June and I have decided to walk up to the church hall, You are welcome to join us if you want to."

Walking up up the tarmac road to the church hall you could feel romance in the air as Martha walked with us.

"George", her pretty face smiling as she spoke. "Fifteen years ago this village was bursting at the seams with volunteers searching for those three missing children. There wasn't a stone they didn't look under. I was hoping in my heart of hearts you would have better luck with your search, and find something the others had missed. But alas, it has revealed nothing. Job Measham wasn't a murderer, he was just a harmless little old man who wouldn't say boo to a goose. His mother and father died young leaving Job's elder brother to look after him. . He too moved out of the area about twenty years ago to get married, leaving poor old Job to fend for himself. Those three young girls were far from angels and made old Job's life a misery. Throwing stones at his window and taunting him. But the hard facts are ... with the evidence that was gathered and collated pointed to Job Measham and there's no getting away from it."

There was no answer to this statement as George looked at Martha.

Inside the church hall flower decorations had been arranged to give the evening a real boost with a splash of colour. Light hearted renderings from famous shows were sung by the choral society, ending the evening with a standing ovation from the congregation.

Leaving the church hall Martha said to George, "June and I would like to visit our parents graves at the back of the church and rearrange some of the flowers. Asking the lads for their approval George said, "It's a lovely evening the walk will do us good, we will come to, if you don't mind"

The old gothic church towering upwards dominated the front view obscuring the church yard at the back. A rose covered old iron gateway was the only access . Pathways between the graves had been well maintained. All weeds and rubbish removed. A freshly dug grave lay open on the side of the path, pointing to it Martha remarked.

"It's the funeral tomorrow of our local Grocer, Ernie Smith who died last Monday from a long illness".

George's face suddenly light up.

"Martha cast your mind back fifteen years to the night the children went missing. Was there a funeral the following day".

Looking puzzled at the last remark she replied, "Yes... I'll show you where the grave is. Our post mistress, Elsie May, she was buried at 9.30 on the Tuesday morning. That's one morning I shall never forget as we all stood paying our last respects the wind and rain lashed our faces like a whip. Branches from two huge Yew trees obscured the tombstones in this corner of the churchyard. In amongst them a white marble stone, on it, Rest In Peace Elsie May. Four feet away a stone wall separating the church yard from a narrow field at the bottom end of Copthorn Woods.

"Fred where is the last place you would expect to find three school children's bodies.?"

He had caught George's drift and answered, "In someone else's grave."

Martha looked alarmed as she spoke to George. "You can't start digging graves up!. If you're hundred percent sure it's time you contacted the proper authorities and gave them all your information."

In the B&B dining room the next morning at breakfast George's face was beaming like a cat who had just found the cream.

June walked in and handed George a letter. "This has just been pushed through the door it's marked, George, I don't know what's happening at Andrew Pearsons small holding there seems a lot of activity, I've seen police cars, and an ambulance racing up there."

Taking the letter off June he began reading it . 'To whom it may concern,' it was a signed confession It's contents held him like a magnet.

'I have lived the last fifteen years of my life with the dread that one day someone would come and discover the truth about the three missing school girls. Watching from a vantage point in the church yard last night my heart sank into my mouth as you inspected Elsie May's grave, I knew there and then the game was up. By the time you have read this letter. I will have paid the price for my cowardice in letting someone else take the punishment for a crime I committed. But don't judge me too harshly, hear my side of the story first. My only son Andrew and his wife and three children came to live in Copthorn about twenty years ago. After spending all his money on his new venture, he persuaded me to sell up and go in shares with him. My wife had died two years previous so I had no ties. Andrew had always been a young lad who puts his heart and soul into any project he takes on. By purchasing this small holding in Copthorn his ambition was to turn it into a garden centre. On the side of the main farm building was a small flat which suited all my requirements giving me free access at any time. My young son has always been a good worker working all hours to provide food and clothes for his family. My daughter in law 'Alice' on the other hand can't even spell the word work. Her day consists of lounging about and driving around the village in her new sports car and chatting to any men she may encounter. On her return home cooking meals was out of the question. Her behaviour being discussed by Andrew and myself on several occasions.

It all came to a head one day when she burst into my room and demanded I leave the small holding. It was then I reminded her I'm not a lodger here, I'm an equal partner. After that discussion with her, things started going from bad to worse. Returning home in the evening from delivering produce for my son my belongings had been strewn across the floor. Tablets I needed for my daily medication gone, even my grandchildren's minds had been poisoned against me. All of this being started by my evil daughter in law. Another story implanted in the children's minds to frighten me, was I"m going to tell every body you have been interfering and molesting us. I couldn't believe my own ears the words coming out of their young mouths; my eldest grandaughter, Jessica aged nine and her two school friends, made my life a living nightmare always going out of their way to cause me trouble demanding money and making fun of me. This again I put down to her mother in her bid to get rid of me. It all came to a head one Monday evening when I saw Job Measham chase the three little hell cats into the woods.

They made a bee line straight for me calling me names and demanding money.

In my bid to escape their taunts I began climbing over the

wall that backed onto one of our fields. The top layers of the wall came away cascading rocks and mortar down. To my horror the three little girls caught the full force of the falling masonry with disastrous results, seeing the extent of the accident and their broken and twisted bodies. My hands would not stop shaking as I picked up their little bodies one by one. Once there evil mother's tongue had done its work I knew no-one would ever believe me. So I decided to bury their bodies in the church yard in the freshly dug grave for Elsie May, the following morning. When the coffin was lowered in it would hide the bodies for ever. One of the little girls shoes must have fell off as I carried the bodies past Job Meashams back gate on the way down the side of the wall to the churchyard. Returning later I rebuilt the damaged wall, never realising in a thousand years an innocent man would be convicted of the crime. Don't judge me too harshly. The only evil perpetrator in this whole sad affair is my evil Daughter in Law... Alice......... Joe Pearson. '

George finished reading the letter just as Martha came bursting into the room.

" One of our neighbours has just Informed me they have just found Joe Pearson's body hanging in the green house at the garden centre".

Handing Martha the letter his answer was, "I know."

*   *   *   *   *

December with its dark and cold miserable days. Fred had just finished clearing away some garden rubbish. When his mind went back to the warm days of the summer especially the one's spent at Copthorn. Sitting down on his swing he began smiling to himself. George had told him a cock and bull story but between them they had unravelled a fifteen year old mystery and cleared an innocent man's name and to top it all, and to make the year complete George and Martha were to be married in the spring, and you know what,! ......he has asked me to be his best man!.

So you know the old saying, all's well that ends well.

THE END

Enemy from the sea

During the blitz on London in World War two, thousands and thousands of school children were evacuated from the danger areas in the city, to the safety of the towns, and villages far away in the countryside. Among this vast migration were identical twin sisters, Carey and Amanda Hitchcock nine years old, both were of average height and build,with lovely brown hazel eyes and long brown hair tied in pigtails that were hanging down their back. It had taken their mother Martha weeks of arguments before she could finally persuade the youngsters to leave home. Finally she could now breathe a sigh of relief as she watched the train transporting them, slowly disappear into a distant tunnel. Martha's elder sister Emily, had consented to have the two girls for the duration of the war. So now they were safely on their way to Cornwall knowing full well in her mind she and her husband could cope with the nightly air raids and help turn the tide of war without worrying about their children.

Smoke from the train's engine billowed up filling the station with a white smog. As they waited patiently on that cold Cornish railway platform. All their worldly and treasured possessions packed into suit cases on the floor by their side's. Passengers hurrying and scurrying passing to and fro from side to side, giving them the occasional glance. Their brown school raincoats and scarves keeping the cold at bay. Suddenly a strong powerful voice broke the silence.

"The last time I saw you two little mites you were both

crawling about on your bellies and you hadn't got a stitch on, now look at you both, my, my, how you have grown. An elderly woman was addressing them. Her lovely brown flashing hazel eyes transfixed on the twins, and as she spoke her face beamed with joy.

"Now which one of you is Carey and which one is Amanda?, only I've bought some black chalk to write your initials on your foreheads least I forget". All the while she was talking she was laughing to herself. "Let me introduce myself, I'm your Aunt Emily". Speaking in a strong Cornish dialect the twin girls had trouble in understanding her strange accent.

"You don't speak anything like our mother", Carey said to her Aunt.

Their aunts face light up with mischief as she answered the twins.

"That's because young madam, your mother and I were split up when we were both young Martha went to live in London with father, and I stayed down here with mother, next question?". All the while she was speaking she had a smile on her face from ear to ear.

"Now come on you two it's starting to get dark. Pick up your cases and follow me your Uncle Sam is waiting outside to take us back to the farm".

As the twins eyed up the strange person now confronting them, they realised she was nothing like their mother. Their aunt was well built, outward going and down to earth. Fashion wasn't one of her strong points for the old waterproof mackintosh and Wellington boots she wore were covered in mud. There was an old brown trilby hat hiding her now greying hair and to top it all. She wore an old red jumper that was covered in chicken feathers. However the warmth in her voice and that twinkle in those mischievous brown eyes, made the twins feel at home straight away.

A stocky man with a round red face and short grey hair sat on a flat based four wheeled cart. He to had a comical side to his character as he started talking to the twins, "I bet you're both cold and hungry after your long journey, young misses?. Never mind I've bought you some nice warm soup".

As he spoke the two girls burst out in laughter. Sam looked at Emily puzzled.

"It's okay Sam", she said smiling back at him, "these two little horrors have been used to a London accent, ours will take some getting used to."

"Now lets see which one of you is the heaviest," as she picked them up and put each one on the cart. "Sam I'm sure I've strained my arm picking them up they both weigh a ton", she said laughing out loud. As the horse clip-clopped down the narrow winding country lanes the scenery was spectacular. The two youngsters bombarded their Aunt with questions about the region. Sam stopping the cart now and then to let the children take a better look at the panoramic views. At one point in their journey he stopped by a dung heap, both girls holding their noses remarked, "what's that terrible smell?".

Sam laughing out loud replied, "that my dears is the smell of the country".

This made the twins howl with laughter, because it was a flat cart there were no seats so the two girls had to stand up and hang on to their Aunts coat. Jogging along at a nice leisurely pace she was asking them various questions about their mother and father and their family life, and also their food likes and dislikes. "I hope you both like cornish pasties, as that is what I've cooked for tea tonight"

"We have never had any", Amanda replied to her aunt

"Well you're in for a treat then young lady".

Shiplade farm, as it was called, was to be their new home for the duration of the war. Perched high up overlooking a narrow winding path and leading down the cliffs to a large sandy cove below. It was a spacious stone built dwelling with a thatched roof, barns and outhouses on the side. It's rugged coast line was like looking at pictures they had seen in books of a smugglers paradise. Huge Atlantic rollers from the open sea came charging in and smashing against the rocks cascading the water upwards.

A red and white lighthouse took pride of place on the edge of the cliffs to warn shipping of the treacherous rocks that lay hidden below the surface of the waves. Their Uncle Sam's job, as well as running his farm, was to keep the lighthouse working in pristine condition.

Carey and Amanda were thrilled to bits with their new accommodation and the room they shared looking out over the sea. As Emily helped the twins unpack their cases she suddenly gave out a yell, "Sam come here quick", responding to her call, she held out in front of her three games in boxes, Ludo, Snakes and Ladders, and Draughts, you now I haven't played these since my childhood. After tea and when I've finished the washing up, I'll get Sam to clear the table then you two are in for a treat'. During the months that followed the twins were starting to adapt to their new way of life, especially helping their Aunt and Uncle about the farm, feeding and looking after the livestock which ranged from, chickens, ducks, geese, pigs sheep and cows. They also helped in the greenhouse which was used for growing tomatoes and market garden produce. Every available piece of land was put to work, growing, wheat, barley, and potatoes to help the war effort.

Being an isolated farm miles from anywhere they didn't get many visitors. So arrangements had to be made about the twins education. Every morning, their Aunt would take them by cart up a narrow winding path to the main road at the top of the farm lane. There they would meet other school children and then walk the remaining one mile to the local village school. Sometimes if they were lucky a passing cart would pick them up and give them a lift into town. Carey and Amanda were both chatter- boxes and had no trouble in finding new friends. Every Friday their Aunt would take them to school picking up their many friends en route. She would then sell her produce at the local market which helped to pay for supplies from the local shop. Emily had a natural flair for conversation and she could make even the simplest things seem funny. This used to amuse the village folk, for when the children's birthday parties came around, with her entertainment skills, she was always the centre of attention.

Saturday night was also a night to remember. It was bath night in front of a blazing hot fire.

Back at home they had a private bathroom and privacy, not so here at the farm. A tin bath was placed in front of the fire, then filled with boiling and cold water to get the right temperature. Aunt Emily took pride of place. She was first, then while she dried herself down with a towel, it was the twins turn, then the two farm dogs, the cat had more sense and she used to run off. This was all followed by a cup of piping hot tea and then followed by a board game or two. You had to make sure you counted off the squares for uncle Sam because he was prone to cheat.

Exploring their new domain one afternoon, the twins wandered by accident down a steep winding slope that led to some caves below the lighthouse. A deep channel had been cut out of the rock caused by the continuous flow of a river flowing out of the cave making its way down to the Sea. Reading books at school about pirates and hidden treasure sent there little minds into a world of fantasy and as their curiosity got the better of them, they ventured inside. A well worn path led them inside to a small marina where two small rowing boats had been moored in a pool cut out by the sea. This made their little minds work overtime thinking of all the stories they had read about smugglers and buried treasure. They ventured even deeper into the cave having the surprise of their lives when they saw electric lights had been installed and there were big wooden boxes stacked on top of one another in rows. They also found covered by some waterproof green sheets some funny pointed cylinder like objects with fins at the blunt end on a series of racks.

Suddenly appearing from behind some rocks, they were challenged by a man in blue overalls, who at once grabbed them by the arm and called for some assistance. Three more men all dressed the same appeared from lower down in the cave, who then began eyeing the two youngsters up very suspiciously. One of the men who seemed to be in charge began winding a telephone and speaking to someone on the other end. They had trouble understanding their Aunts accent, but they couldn't understand a word these men spoke. After what seemed like a lifetime their Aunt showed up her face beaming with a smile as usual.

"You two had me worried sick, I thought you had met with an accident, I've been looking everywhere for you, thank God you're both safe. Come on now it's time for your tea, say goodbye to your friends".

Emily looked at them both with a serious expression on her face, " girls in these troubled times, with the war going on,careless talk can sink ships, so promise me you will not breathe a word of this encounter to anyone. Is that understood.?"

They both nodded in agreement.

Sam used to play with the twins a lot. He was a very strong man and a game they both enjoyed to play was where each girl would hang on to his wrists. He would then spin them around and around sending the two girls legs flying up in the air like a merry go round at the fair.

On their arrival at school on Friday morning their Aunt had a discussion with the headteacher. "Those two little scamps had Sam and myself running around in circles last night with their fairy stories. They said they had seen some funny men in the caves below the light house. You know what children are like with their over active imaginations I told them it was probably the Cornish pixies. Later Sam and myself went down to investigate and found nothing". Emily's comical explanation of last nights events was so convincing that the village folk looked on the two youngsters as having wild and vivid imaginations.

Passing the lighthouse one day while out exploring the twins noticed someone had left the door open. Peeking inside, they decided to go in and climb the steps to the top. Half way up on a small landing was a room on the side with bars on the door. Imprisoned inside a man and woman who resembled their Aunt and uncle in both looks and build.

Looking through the bars Carey and Amanda began talking to the two inmates," What have you done so wrong to be locked up in here".

The woman came walking over to the bars and on seeing the two little girls broke down in a flood of tears.

"You're Martha's two daughters Carey and Amanda I'd know you anywhere you are just like your mother. Uncle Sam and I are being held prisoners by German agents that have taken over our farm. This isn't a fairy story, please, please, believe me. I'm your real Aunt Emily the other two are impostors. They intend using the caves below for storage and the light from the lighthouse to signal their U boats moored out at sea to attack our shipping convoys. The two agents posing as uncle Sam and me are very convincing talkers, but you must get someone to believe you. It's a matter of life and death. Please try and get help before its too late. Now go quickly and be careful you're not seen."

Carey and Amanda were able to slip out of the light house door without being seen. Reaching a place of safety both decided on a plan of strategy of telling the village constable their story. Both of them had been branded as having wild exaggerated imaginations, so their quest would not be an easy one.

Bert Pollock the village constable listened to the young girls story feeling very uneasy and with great doubts in his mind. He didn't relish the idea of being made a fool of in front of the whole village by two young strangers. So he decided his best course of action would be to take the youngsters back and confront their Aunt and Uncle with this news and see their reactions. Emily as usual had all the answers ready for his many questions just as though the whole episode was part of a carefully planned operation and even giving him a guided tour of the lighthouse. There was no one inside. Smiling at the two girls and at the constable, "You two with your wild exaggerated stories will be the death of me yet. I'm sorry they have wasted your time Pc Pollock but would a nice cup of tea and a piece of home made cake make up for your wasted journey?". Their Aunts wit and charm and the way she could manipulate words had turned a very serious accusation into a laughable incident. Constable Pollock's report simply read, incident investigated but the young girls were prone to making up fairy stories.

Several days later an old man arrived in the village inquiring about a distant relative who had lived there many years ago. He was trying to trace his kin folks there abouts. Many of the village folk judged him by his clothes and wild actions regarded him as an old tramp and paid him no heed. He was a tall slim built man with a mop of grey hair, some hanging down the side of his face, with the rest hidden by an old trilby hat. His tattered clothes had seen better days, and a pair of thick horn rimmed glasses, hid a wrinkled weathered face. His appearance and his dress sense didn't match his well spoken accent, so one can only assume he was some old eccentric from the past.

Walking back from school one day the twins came across this strange old man walking down the lane leading down to the farm. He introduced himself to them as professor Albert Ingram. He told them his hobby was bird watching. This statement amused the two girls because the old man couldn't see more then a few yards in front of him without falling over. When he walked he would slip and stagger and fall over objects. Hearing their childish laughter of disbelief he explained to them he could listen to the birds calls and tell them exactly what bird it was. Meeting someone who spoke in the same accent as themselves and could converse on any subject made the two girls listen to his funny sense of humour, and his vast knowledge and expertise on wild birds. Carey and Amanda were thrilled to bits with their new found friend, arranged to meet the old man at the very same spot the following day. This time they were accompanied by their Aunt Emily who was very curious about their new found friend. When the old man eventually turned up he had trouble in negotiating the winding paths due to his poor eyesight. Emily at once got on the offensive questioning him thoroughly about his bird watching practice. The ferocity of her interrogation got too much for the old man, who broke down and told the three of them his sad story.

"I've spent the past ten years in an old people's home having been diagnosed with a terminal illness. My doctors realised my plight and there was nothing more they could do so they released me. I wanted to spend what time I had left pursuing my favourite hobby, bird watching. Even as the old man spoke his eyes were focused on Emily. "Your accent and the way you speak reminds me of a young girl that used to live around these parts. In my bygone years I've spent many happy hours with her exploring the cliffs and caves around here".

Emily listened to the old man's stories until she was convinced there was no harm in him. She then gave him permission to meet the twins again and carry on with his bird watching. Over the next few days the two girls would arrange to meet the old man and take him some food and guide him safely over the rocky terrain while he pursued his favourite hobby.

On the Saturday morning of that particular week the two girls were awakened from their slumber by the sound of gun fire, an aircraft flying low and explosions coming from the direction of the lighthouse. Both girls in a sheer panic went running down stairs to see what was happening only to see the farm house door suddenly burst open and three soldiers rushing inside pointing guns at Emily and Sam, followed by Professor Ingram brandishing a pistol.

"You two, the games up, you are both under arrest. Your two U boats out in the bay have been sunk and your men in the caves captured. Also our commando assault team have released the childrens real Aunt Emily and Uncle Sam. All your scheming and lies were of no avail. Our intelligent services had pinpointed a possible area your U boats were operating from all we needed was confirmation of the exact site. The strange irony of it all is that you nearly got away with it".

"Having these two young girls thrust on you by their parents must have been a shock in it's self. But I must say in all fairness you played your parts well".

"If it hadn't have been for the intelligence and patriotism of the two young schoolgirls you would have remained undetected for years killing thousands of innocent people with your acts of barbarism. In your smugness and arrogance you had allowed them to write home to their Mom and Dad once a week who were vetting each letter. The two of them had worked out a foolproof system which even you could not detect. Their father worked for the special branch,decoding messages. On his very rare weekends off, before the twins were evacuated he would pass away the hours playing with them using special words in sentences to denote danger. Each girl was given permission by you to write home to their parents once a week, one letter by itself was just childish nonsense, but put the two together with the code sign and they told a different story, telling of the strange goings on down here. That's when my department was contacted and instructed me to investigate the said incidents."

The End

OLD NELLIE the steam engine

Many isolated towns and villages were completely cut off in the 1960s,when the Beeching axe fell and closed all the branch railway lines which were feeding these small local communities. One such line in particular felt the brunt of the closure. The 20 mile stretch that spurred off from Norbury Junction, on the main western line which then ran through some of the most picturesque country side in England. With breath taking panoramic views, passing through five stations would continue en-route to the seaside town of Mablethorpe. It's single line rail track was used six times a day,as it's aging rolling stock delivered everything from passengers, to livestock, milk, and heavy freight. In the early part of the twentieth century it was decided to build a branch line from Norbury Junction to link up all the small towns to Mablethorpe. Construction gangs began carving out the route by cutting a path through a large steep sided ravine and then digging a tunnel fifty yards long in the hillside. This then opened up onto a large metal bridge spanning the River Mab estuary. Then it would continue along the coast another three miles terminating at Mablethorpe.

This small corner of England could boast about it's railway. It opened up a whole new way of life for them, by letting in tourism to explore it's many beauty spots and also sample the excellent fishing in the area. In the 1960s like a thunder bolt out of the blue, the sad news came that the rail spur was to close. A brave attempt was made by the local people and railway enthusiasts to get fund raising schemes started to try and save the line and it's rolling stock. This gesture was well supported and helped them buy and secure the 20 mile single track, leaving them with little money to carry out vital maintenance work.   -

George Jarvis now well into his seventies had driven the old pannier-tank railway engine nicknamed "OLD NELLIE' all of his working life until his retirement. News of the closure had devastated him. This little railway line was like the life giving blood in his arteries. It was part of his life. Everyone knew him, and he in turn knew every solitary person down that old railway line, giving three loud blasts on the engine's horn as he passed outlying farms and cottages. His sudden death was bought on by the traumatic events and stress of the closure, and he bequeathed all his life savings including the sale of his house,to be placed at the disposal of the railway enthusiast's committee. This was to try and save the little railway and it's engine and rolling stock from the scrap yard and developers; His dream was that if enough money could be donated, then one day,'Old Nellie' would once again chug up and down the tracks between Norbury Junction and Mablethorpe carrying, freight and passengers just like in the olden days.

His two grown daughter's Jessie, and Elsie, with the aid of some friends and relatives had sold all they had including their own houses, to try and make their late father's dream come true. With the money raised from the sales they then purchased the branch line railway station at Norbury Junction. Both sister's had invested everything they had on a dream. Their intention was to turn the the old railway station into a restaurant and transport cafe with accommodation facilities for paying guests. A large car park at the entrance to the old railway station would provide them with ample parking. Plans had also been drawn up to build additional living accommodation for both Jessie, and Elsie's families. They knew the area had a lot to offer with it's fishing and it's scenic beauty so the two sisters were gambling upon good wholesome food, clean rooms and beds, and plenty of good old fashioned fresh air to entice the tourists into the railway station facilities. A drink's licence had been granted, the idea being to use the transport cafe in the work-days and open the restaurant for Saturday and Sunday lunches.

Jessie, at 55, was the older of the two sisters and a widow. Her husband Ralph had died of a brain tumour five years ago. He too had once worked on the railway. Their only child of the marriage, a daughter called Jody, had met and married a young man while she was at college and now lived with her husband and young son in America.

Elsie was four years younger than Jessie. Both had the same common interest and a bubbly personality, and to see them out you couldn't tell them apart. They both had short black hair with a fringe at the front, blue sparkling eyes normally hidden by a pair of spectacles, a lovely round face and a cute little button nose. Both girls were well built having well rounded figures.

On the left hand side of the old railway station was a piece of grass land, which Elsie's husband Fred intended turning into a market garden. This would also supply the restaurant with fresh vegetables. Another part of his plans had been to introduce some poultry so that there would be a fresh supply of new laid eggs. Their plans for the future had been made and they were now past the point of no return. There was no going back. It was a case now of fulfilling their destiny, and making their late fathers' dream turn into a reality.

'Old Nellie' and the remaining rolling stock, comprising of one passenger coach, a flat truck, freight car and a guards van, had been shunted onto a siding which ran parallel with the branch line. Volunteers were doing their best to keep out the elements, wind, rain and snow, by placing sheets over all the vital parts on the rolling stock with the hope that one day sufficient funds could be found to overhaul the lot. Everybody engaged on the project was living in hopes and keeping their fingers crossed that the two sisters could pull something out of the bag. Hoping that one day a benefactor would come forward and save the old engine. Funds were needed desperately to get 'Old Nellie' completely overhauled with a new boiler and bearings fitted. Alternatively the heart breaking truth would be, that she would be sold together with the existing rolling stock and broken up for scrap.They had been given a three year dead-line to raise the appropriate capital.

Jessie and Elsie were both excellent cooks and the idea of turning the old railway station into a cafe, and restaurant, was turning out to be a money spinner. People were coming from miles around to sample their cooking. Bookings for the weekends had to be made well in advance to be sure of a table. Their weekday trade lorry drivers, were telephoning in from miles away with their orders for breakfasts and lunches, making special detours to enable them to get a meal at the station cafe. A lot of the local motor bike fraternity were also using the cafe as their base, all helping to build up trade.

With the restaurant and cafe trade booming more volunteers had also been recruited to help maintain the old railway engine and rolling stock. They were all being spurred on with the promise of a free sample of the two sisters cooking. Elsie had two teenage daughter's Tracy, and Sarah,who had both been recruited to help their mom and aunt turn the old railway station cafe/ restaurant into a gold mine. Jessie and her little band of helpers had their own kind of jovial personality, wit and charm,and could handle any situation in any form, especially being teased by the many lorry drivers that used the cafe. In a lot of cases due to bad weather conditions, stranded lorry drivers who knew they could always count on the two sisters for accommodation plus an excellent breakfast, Jessie and Elsie hadn't got the faces or bodies of film stars but what they had got made up for it double. A willing way, friendly smile and hearts of gold, nothing was too much trouble.

Fred's small market garden was also beginning to pay it's way, selling it's produce to the passing trade and keeping the cafe well stocked up with fresh vegetables.

One morning after the breakfast rush had died away, Jessie noticed one of the biking lads, Alvin sitting on a table by himself, a letter in his hands his eyes full of tears. She went walking over and sat down beside him, " What 's the matter Alvin?" she asked.

"My girlfriend Lisa and her family have moved down to Kent to live. This letter arrived in the post this morning from her telling me she wasn't very happy down there and was having trouble finding new friends. Jessie I have this strange feeling inside that I shall never see again".he blurted out with tear filled eyes.

"How long have you been courting this girl Alvin ? ," Jessie inquired.

"Two and a half years", came his reply.

"So you're just going to sit there day after day feeling sorry for yourself and let someone else steal your girl from you?. Faint heart never won fair lady, what are you, a man or a mouse?".

He was taken back by her blunt remarks " You're right Jessie, I'm going to ride down to Kent and ask Lisa to marry me. That's what I'm going to do!"

"That's more like it !", said Jessie tapping him on the shoulder. "You're not going anywhere on an empty stomach, Elsie bring me a full breakfast over here", she shouted out to her sister.

As the two of them watched his bike disappear down the winding country lane, Elsie said," what's wrong with him?,"

"That young man's in love", she answered her sister smiling.

Four miles down the line from the railway station was an old dis-used quarry, which had recently re-opened, finding work for many local people in the area. It's aim was to supply hard core for a new road building project that was being carried out twenty five miles away. One morning a very smartly dressed gentleman came in for breakfast and approached the two sisters with an offer they couldn't resist. He wanted to rent the branch railway line on behalf of his company for two years and supply the new road builders with hard core from his quarry. As he explained he intended using an old disused spur from the branch line,it's tracks going down a siding into the quarry. Their engineers would test and replace any faulty rails on the old line going to Norbury Junction before it then joined the main western line. A diesel train would be used with forty trucks to transport the hard core on a twenty four hour shift system, to a railway siding twenty five miles away. Then by adding huge hoppers and a conveyor belt, fill up all waiting lorries that were being used on the new road project. After hearing his plans for their small rail link, the two sisters jumped at his offer. They knew in their hearts it would mean more trade for their cafe, but also extra funding to repair their aging rolling stock.

It's surprising the way the years pass by so quickly. Two years had now passed, the new road finished and with it the quarry closure. Twelve men had been left there to finish tidying up the site before they locked up and left it for good .

It had been a terrible wet and windy March day with thunder and lightning and driving rain. Dark overcast skies were making visibility very poor. So the two sister's decided to finish work early on this particular day through lack of customers. As they were about to go through the cafe door and lock up, the telephone rang.

"Jessie, it's Joe Pritchard from the quarry. There's been a terrible accident. An explosion set off by the lightning has caught most of the work force in the blast. Injured and dying men are scattered all over the ground. It looks like something from a war movie. Some of them look in a very critical condition we need help right away. It's a matter of life and death, even the walking wounded are walking about in a daze and in no fit state to cope with this situation. I've tried ringing the main hospital at Mablethorpe but the roads are all washed out due to the heavy deluge of rain and floods and there's no way of getting any ambulances down to us.

Jessie I know it's asking a lot in these appalling conditions but do you think, 'Old Nellie' could be steamed up and save the day?. It's our only hope. Everywhere is flooded and if we don't get help to some of these poor men they will surely die !".even as he spoke his voice kept breaking down with emotion.

" Joe leave it to me',Jessie answered him," I will ring around and get some volunteers to help me." Over the past weekends the old engine had been steamed up, oiled, and greased, to keep her working parts free.

'How about a engine driver"? Joe asked

"You have got one,..... Me, I could drive that old engine

51

blindfolded" she answered him. "When I was young I used to go up and down the tracks with my old dad. I've driven Nellie on numerous occasions so don't worry. Get as many of the men to the top of the siding and then I can reverse down with the volunteers and pick them all up?.

Elsie tugged at Jessie's arm "how about a stoker for the engine'.

'I've got one !.......YOU !'"

Jessie's volunteers with the help of crowbars, sweat , blood and tears and heavy lifting tackle,working in appalling weather conditions managed to get the old engine steamed up, and coupled up to it's rolling stock, ready to roll.

Jessie leaned out of the cab,she hadn't had time to change she was still wearing her apron.

"Fred ! Ring up Joe at the quarry and tell him we are on our way. I will give him three short bursts on the horn to warn him I'm reversing down the siding. By the way, Elsie's shovelling this coal onto the fire like a good one, I"ll soon slim her down to a nice round size ten for you," she laughed out loud.

'Old Nellie' puffed and panted as the strong gale force winds and rain battered her rusty old steel work. Her wheels sparking and screaming out loud as she negotiated the rusty old tracks down the quarry siding. The sight that met their eyes through the driving rain was like a scene from a bombing raid. Injured men lay moaning and groaning all over the ground as the arduous task began for the volunteers to quickly collect them up and load them aboard the awaiting rolling stock.

"That's the last one Jessie" Joe said, having trouble trying to stand up in the driving rain," you can go now". I will telephone the hospital at Mablethorpe and tell them you are on your way."

Jessie gave three short sharp pulls on the horn to warn one of the volunteers at the end of the siding to switch the points to allow them to enter the branch line. Wiping the dripping sweat from her brow Jessie pushed the throttle forward and the old engine began puffing up smoke through its stack.

'Old Nellie's' pistons were forcing out steam at an incredible rate as the old engine made it's way up the track. Some of the rails hadn't been used for years. The wheels creaked squealed and shuddered as they went over the joints in the rails. Jessie was taking no undue risks going at a nice leisurely pace as they approached the steep sided ravine before entering the tunnel she dare not go any faster as the strain on the old engine could cause her boiler to blow up. What happened next frightened the two ladies half to death. There was a almighty crack of thunder, followed by twisted forked lighting striking the top of the steep sided ravine. Then there was a deafening ear piercing roar,cascading rocks and debris down on them.

Elsie screamed out at Jessie at the top of her voice,"Its a landslide open up the throttle quick and give her all she has got, or we shall all be buried alive !".

On that command from her sister she pushed the throttle forward with all her might, knowing in her mind that if the landslide didn't get them, then the old engine's boiler certainly would. As falling rocks and debris bounced off the engine and carriages; it raced into the safety of the tunnel spewing out steam and smoke everywhere making it impossible to see.

Once inside, Jessie began groping blindly in the darkness to ease back on the throttle and to slow down the old engine. The next obstacle in their path was the old iron bridge spanning the river Mab estuary. This meant crossing at a snails pace or ending up in the now flooded river. Inch by inch Jessie negotiated the joints in the rails, as the old engine's wheels squealed rolling over the rusty track that hadn't been used in years. Flood water was lapping at the old rails as they bent and bowed under the weight. Using all her concentration and skills to get the old engine over the bridge safely, she hadn't noticed her sister slumped against the side of the cab blood pouring out from a cut on the top of her head. She couldn't do much to assist her as the station was now in sight. Struggling with the engines controls,she helped 'Old Nellie' limp into Mablethorpe station, steam was pouring out of every loose bolt and nut as she came to a dramatic stop at the station's platform. A fleet of ambulances lost no time in ferrying the injured men to hospital. 'Old Nellie's' piston's finally gave up the ghost rocking the engine violently as they blew up filling the station with steam and smoke. Leaning over to assist her sister she felt a sharp pain at the top of her left leg. As she bent down,she noticed blood was pouring out of a deep cut from a piece of metal that was embedded in it. Everything suddenly went black.

*   *   *   *   *

Sixteen months later after spending a long time in hospital and after countless operations, sometimes in a 50-50 drama, and at one period during her confinement staff were frightened she may lose her left leg. However thanks to the exceptional skills of the nursing staff, they finally won the battle in the end. On a bright sunny Sunday morning in July she was discharged from hospital. Elsie and Fred helped Jessie as she limped out of the hospital ward, and down the corridor to the outside. Patients and staff were saying goodbye to their friend of many months as Jessie clung on tightly to her sisters arm. Driving back home though the country lanes, she was repeatedly bombarding her sister about the fate of the the old Railway engine. Finally to be told in a sympathetic way what had happened.

"I'm sorry Jessie but Old Nellie making that mercy dash all those months away was too much for the old girl. She has finally given up the ghost. That was definitely her last journey" she was told.

Tears welled up in Jessie's eyes. "That was my Dad's and Ralph's dream. That one day the old engine would once again go puffing up and down those tracks from Norbury Junction to Mablethorpe, but I can see by your remarks this will never happen now" she sighed.

Reaching the Old railway station she was amazed at the amount of cars on the car park. Then an even bigger thrill as she opened the station restaurant door. A banner hung from the ceiling with words painted on it in bold red letters, 'Welcome home Jessie' Then a rapturous welcome by relatives and friends. Among them her daughter Jody with husband and her grandson.

Her eyes were flooding out tears at the welcoming sight. Men injured in the quarry blast were their with there families. Some still bearing the scars of their ordeal. One young woman broke down in tears as she thanked Jessie for saving her husbands life. After enjoying a refreshing cup of tea and eating a prepared meal. Elsie led her sister by the hand to the door leading out onto the station platform. A huge curtain had been draped across the door. You could hear a pin drop on the floor, and as she pushed aside the curtain and opened the door to let her sister through.

Jessie stopped dead in her tracks at the sight that met her eyes. Directly in front of her, letting off steam and puffing away merrily in the station. Coupled up to a mighty castle class engine, was 'Old Nellie'. The rust over the years had all gone and was replaced by green paint. Her brass pipes gleaming in the sun's ray's and her name was painted on a metal plate on the sides of the engine in gold letters, 'OLD NELLIE', with the words underneath. 'Pride of the valley', the rolling stock had also received a face lift. Everything glistened as if it were new. Tears flowed from Jessie's eyes as she limped over and patted the old engine. Big Ted,one of Jessie's lorry driver friends, tears pouring down his face presented her with a big bouquet of flowers. "This is a welcoming home present from me and the lads", as he kissed her gently on the cheek, " and once again I say this for everyone gathered here today. Welcome home Jessie".

Her sister explained her epic mercy dash had caused a great deal of publicity. Lots of well wishers from all around the country on reading the story had donated money to save the old railway engine. Also, a steam preservation society, on hearing the good news of Jessie's release from hospital, had loaned them the castle class engine for the weekend. Elsie took Jessie by the hand and with tears filling her eyes she spoke to her sister. "Through our efforts and hard work we have made our Dad's dream come true. Somewhere up there he is looking down on us with pride ".

One of the engine drivers shouted down to her "Madam climb aboard your carriage awaits. There's a bottle of chilled champagne waiting for you, so relax and enjoy the journey. Oh, and Jessie, on behalf of all the people gathered here today, Welcome back home". Both engines gave three long blasts on their horns as smoke was forced out of their smoke stacks they went thundering out of the station, amid the cheering and banner waving.

"Next stop Mablethorpe!". shouted the guard.

THE END

Legend of The Little Red Hen

On a visit to our local church yard recently, to lay a floral tribute on a loved ones' grave, I felt ashamed as I looked at the broken marble stone crosses and figures. Once items to be admired, and now lying on the ground damaged beyond repair. Staring down at the grave my eyes became glued to an inscription on a stone water vase. Wind and rain had worn away most of the writing but, I could just make out the message ; In loving memory of Luke Dunn, and the date 1936. A remarkable story had been told to me, many many years ago, concerning this particular plot, for also sharing the grave with Luke was a racing pigeon. Stories like this, if not recorded or written down are lost forever. All those many years ago I made a solemn vow that one day I would put pen to paper and would write this very unusual true story.

Feats of heroism and bravery beyond the call of duty are normally attributed to the exploits of man, so it must feel very strange indeed reading a story about one of our feathered friends. In fact, a little red hen, a racing pigeon . Luke Dunn was the proud owner of a flock of racing pigeons. White one's with blue and black markings, different shades of blue one's with white markings, and red ones. Attending to their every whim all his spare time in the day,was attributed to keeping them well fed, exercised, and watered, trained to the limit and in tip top condition. This was his life's work. Another one of his proud possession's found at the top of a brick built walled narrow garden and In the middle of towering factory chimneys and buildings which was in the industrial Black Country, was his white washed pigeon pen. This was to house his pride and joy, his beloved pigeons. It was that clean inside you could eat your meals of it's floor. Nesting boxes ran along it's back wall, all kept in pristine condition, and a black and white painted door was at the front to loose his birds in and out.

Springtime was a particular busy time of the year for him getting his pigeons trained for the months ahead in preparation, for the racing pigeon season which was now in full swing. Pigeons were sent in their baskets by train to various locations. At first, to destinations that were near at hand, where they were released and timed on the homeward journey. Then as they progressed in their training programme the distances got further and further away. Excitement filled the air, for this very weekend he had selected one of his pigeons, (in fact his pride and joy, a little red hen who he hoped would do him proud), to fly in a race that would be started in France. All the pigeons that were taking part in the race were being shipped in big pigeon baskets and sent to the French mainland to be released at a specific time. The return journey back home included flying across the French main land, then the open sea, before finally arriving back home in record time and winning the race. Carefully selecting a bird out of his flock to undertake such a perilous journey, he had chosen the little red hen who in past races had proven her worth. Another key factor in her favour was that she was about to be a mother, with her two white eggs ready to chip out any day and so he was sure she wouldn't lose any time in coming back.

To enter the race and make it official a rubber ring was attached to her leg with a number on it. This was to indicate what club she belonged to. As the pigeon baskets were loaded aboard the waiting transporter Luke watched as the pigeons billed and cooed in their new surroundings A little tear trickled down his cheek as he saw the transports finally disappearing down the distant road.

Arriving back home that evening his fist job was to make sure that the little red hens mate, a blue cock bird, was doing his duty and sitting on her clutch of eggs keeping them warm as they were due to hatch out at any time. He knew through his own racing pigeon experience that she wouldn't waste any time in getting home to see the arrival of her first new born chicks into the world.

Saturday morning at the start of the pigeon race all the time clocks were checked and recorded. Even the weather smiled favourably down on them it was a beautiful sunny day with hardly a breeze blowing. Feathers and dust were flying about in all directions in that little French village . As the signal was given to open the baskets and release the pigeons, the atmosphere was alive as thousands of flapping wings took to the air, for a brief instance blotting out the light from the sun , as they flew around and around, to get their bearings for their journey back home. Flying over the French countryside exercising their little wings must have seemed like heaven after being transported in those cramped baskets for so long.

With a tail wind blowing in their favour and the sun shining out of a clear blue sky, there shouldn't be any problems as they would do the crossing in record time. Thousands of pigeons flew over the picturesque towns, and villages, casting a dark shadow on the ground below them, then over open fields of maize, wheat and barley, making their way towards the French coast and the open sea.

A day that had started so full of promise was about to end. On reaching the open sea even the stoutest of hearts must have looked in despair at what lay in front of them. The sky of blue and a gentle tail breeze that they had enjoyed so much on their first lap of the journey had now turned a complete cycle. They were now faced with pitch black darkness as the storm clouds raced in from the Atlantic blocking their path. They were in an impossible situation and there was no way around it. This dramatic weather pattern and change of events had not been forecast by the weather men and caught everyone off guard. Strong winds and driving rain had whipped the sea up into a frenzy as mountainous waves cascaded white spray upwards and tore along the shore line like a tidal wave. What chance did their frail little bodies stand in such a predicament as they flew straight into the heart of the storm?. Frantically flapping their wings, as the strong winds and driving rain tossed them up and down, to and fro, then from side to side, flying a straight course was an impossible task. Every ounce of strength was being sucked out of them as they battled against overwhelming odds in that terrible storm to reach land and safety. Claps of deafening thunder making the heavens shake and shudder as it rolled, sheet lightning lighting up the skyline. Where once there was many the storm had begun to take it's toll. Pigeons' growing weary from the strain, were plummeting down like stones into the raging waters below. The little red hen had braved natures elements were many had failed, but the crossing wasn't over yet. She knew in her heart of hearts that at any moment a huge wave could rise up and drag her down to the sea's murky depths. Feathered friends once flying side by side, one by one had disappeared from sight, leaving her to face the journey alone. A glimpse of land on the distant horizon made her little wings beat faster, it must have seemed like a miracle after facing the perils of that death defying crossing. Blown many miles off course she must now pick up familiar landmarks, like beacons, to guide her safely back home. Floating about in the sea below were little feathered bodies being tossed about by the waves. Many had started the crossing but now there were but a few to complete the journey.

Worried owners back home on hearing the alarming news on the radio about the terrible storm, paced their gardens relentlessly. Eyes scanning the skies looking for any tell tale signs of hope that at least one of their birds had got through. Luke's eyes were filled with tears as he nervously paced the garden. His theory was 'where there's life there's hope'. Being joined by other pigeon fanciers who were all giving their own opinions of what had happened on that terrible sea crossing. He was only half listening to their tales of woe, as his eyes strained to see up into that now darkening evening sky.   In his own mind he knew that if the little red hen didn't come in the next few minutes she wouldn't be coming at all.   Walking into his pigeon pen he began gently stroking and soothing the cock bird, as the eggs he was sitting on were beginning to hatch out. Speaking in a very emotional voice he said, "Have faith my little beauty, if there's a way through, she will find it ." The truth of the matter was only too plain to see. The little red hen's time was beginning to run out. Just then one of his friends in the garden gave out a yell you could hear a mile away.

" Look up there........ just passing that tall chimney stack above the factory roofs, that little black dot, it's coming straight for us". Luke raced out of his pigeon pen half stumbling and half walking in his excitement to see what all the commotion was about. Eyes straining to see in that now darkening sky,he was just in time to see his little red hen, wings outstretched soaring through the open door and straight on to her nest just in time to see her first born arrive into the world. Old Luke was so overcome with emotion that the tears were streaming down his face as he looked at his little bird now tending to her young. She had achieved an almost impossible task by flying through the storm of the century. Ushering all his friends out of the pen with a few kind words.

" That little bird deserves her moment of glory and a good night's rest so let's leave her in peace with her new born chicks" .

When news of her return got out the next day, all hell broke loose as people came from miles around to gaze at this wonder of nature. A story of this magnitude spread like wild fire around the towns and villages about the little red hen's astounding achievement. Old Luke felt ten feet tall as he told the people congregated there about her final home coming. He gently cradled the little hen in his hands. "She came out of the night sky like a rocket, flying through the open pigeon pen door, straight onto her eggs just in time to see the first one hatch out ". Listening to his story tears were rolling down even the hardest of faces. Luke died in the winter of that year and his little red hen died four years later. Through someone's noble gesture they had buried the little bird in the same grave as her master finally reuniting them both in death.

This is a true story that had been told to me by a woman who had witnessed the whole event. This was based on facts as they had happened however over the years exact dates and times had been lost.

THE END

My Journal

All of my life I have kept a journal on important times and dates in my life. Like going to a friend's or relation's birthday party, seeing a pop concert or going on an important journey, it all makes good reading. It's a book giving an accurate account of my life, and also it's many pages incidents in it can be related too, as I live my life to the full. Time waits for no one, being once told. If records are not kept you have a tendency to forget, taking all this into account. My journal began. My name is Carol Rowe. I'm forty seven years old, married to my husband Mike and have two teenage boys, Craig and Billy. Looking after them all, now that is a full time job in itself. I still manage to snatch the time off now and again and make notes and scribble a few things in my journal. A lot of my close friends keep diaries also keeping a track of every day events in their lives. There are periods in our daily routine when you may have time to kill, so turning over the pages in my journal reading about an event that happened in my life many years ago even now, looking back, the very thought of it makes me shudder.

    I was twelve when my dear old dad gave me this journal to keep as a record of my life's achievements. From time to time entries could be made in it depicting the important stages in my life and as I grew into woman hood. Hoping it would recompense and smooth the waters for the shock that my dad was about to spring on me. Working at a big engineering firm one day he had been approached by the board room staff and asked if he would be interested in starting a new branch of the company in North America,with an increase in salary and all expenses paid. My father talked over the idea with my mother, who at once agreed knowing full well this could be their golden opportunity.The only fly in the ointment,!   being me. Arrangements were hastily made for me to go and live with my Aunt May and Uncle Ben and my two cousins in a little place called Danly, on the Welsh border. It would only be on a temporary basis, just until my mom and dad could find their feet in his new position and return to England and take me back with them to America. This all sounded too good to be true, as one cold winter's morning I started my new life, finding myself walking up my aunt's garden path with all my belongings in a suitcase. She was on the doorstep to greet me.

"Come on young lady, let's get you bedded down and settled in shall we?".

Aunt May was a big well built woman with a lovely round face and a mop of curly blonde hair. Her family consisted of my cousin Claire, who was the same age as me and a younger version of her mother, her younger brother Robert, ten was slight in build with black hair. My Uncle Ben was five years my father's senior and a miner, where my father was slim built, he was broad and big boned and a mountain of a man. For all his size he had his own comical little way's that used to amuse me and make me laugh.They welcomed me with open arms into their family and we all got on like an house on fire.

Turning over the pages and reading through the notes in my journal, while enjoying my stay with my aunt and uncle, I recalled an incident to mind that could have been written for a sci -fi horror film. It all began in the month of February after I had been a house guest at their home for the last two months.

Whilst my cousins and I were returning home from school one day, to the house on a small housing estate, consisting of approximately one hundred and fifty houses all with open planned lawns at the front. The area around the estate was mainly wooded with hills in the background actually forming a secluded valley.

With the freak weather conditions at this time of the year, we were actually experiencing a mini heat wave in the middle of February. This day in particular was quite warm and therefore we were walking with our winter coats over our arm's instead of wearing them. A very dull overcast sky appeared above and felt as though someone was holding a giant magnifying glass over the clouds catching the sun's heat rays and beaming it in a straight line at our tiny corner of the world. It was very overpowering. Then a strange thing suddenly happened. Without any warning, the sky went as black as night sending the temperature plummeting we were bombarded with hail stones as big as marbles which only lasted about five minutes and then it all went quiet again. Experiencing the two extremes of weather conditions in such a short space of time made headline news in the press and on the T .V. However all the stories telling of this strange occurrence, had one thing in common. It was only happening in a one mile radius of my uncle and aunt's house at Danly. No one could offer an explanation for this strange weather pattern.

Telephone calls from my Mom and Dad came on a regular basis. We would swap gossip I told them about our strange weather conditions. In turn dad would tell me the progress they were both making. From the sound of my mother's voice on the telephone, she was getting home sick.Uncle Ben fancied himself as a singing star and so every Saturday night we walked about a mile to the next village, to the Miner's Welfare club. Looking back over the years at some of his antics when he was drunk made me laugh so much I used to wet myself. His favourite song was'Delilah', you might say that it was the highlight of the evening, and we all joined in the chorus singing at the top of our voices. Returning home from the club on this particular Saturday night, it was the last week in April, walking back in the moonlight, someone had grown a small privet hedge bordering their property on one the older houses in the area, there In amongst the leaves were four large caterpillars the like of which I had never seen before . They were about four inches long and had a shiny black back with an orange strip covering both sides of their body. Two distinctive little lumps were sticking up at the front, which I assumed were their eyes. They had a fluorescent green forked tail and were covered sparsely in bright green fluorescent hair. I stared at these strange caterpillars in amazement because never before had I seen anything like them. My first instinct was to reach out and touch one, but a shout from my aunt May made me withdraw my hand immediately. "Don't touch them, you don't know what they are or where they have come from". Recalling the event now, that shout came in the nick of time saving me from a fate worse then death. On the Monday morning the whole of school attended a church service in the main assembly hall, there the head master bought up the subject of these giant caterpillars. He mentioned the fact that some of the pupils, and their parents, had foolishly handled them, and as a result, their hands were covered in a dark purple rash and blisters. So he emphasised the point very strongly again until more could be found out about these strange insects if you do happen to see any on your travels don't touch them and leave well alone. Returning back home from school that day with my cousins and pointing at the privet hedge where last night we had seen four caterpillars, now there were seven all munching away at the green leaves.

On our arrival at my aunt's house that evening my aunt was immediately informed about our head master's lecture and words of advice were she responded with another quote from the past.

"Your grandmother always impressed on us girls when we were young. If you are not quite sure, what it is, or where it has come from, then leave it alone and that's my advice to you three". Every morning walking to and fro from school was like living in a nightmare. Everywhere you looked these weird looking caterpillars were devouring all the green foliage in sight, like a swarm of hungry locusts. Some had fallen victim to passing cars by walking in the road under the wheels of cars, their remains left a tell tale sign of horror, a bright green gungy mess. If you examined it closely it started to bubble up as though its content's contained some kind of acid. It was horrible. We were told by some of our school friends, that they had stepped on some by accident. The results were catastrophic. The green gunge had eaten away at the soles and heels on their shoes. Also one of our friend's had remarked his father had trodden on one in the dark while going up the garden and when returning back to the house, had walked across the carpet and where his foot had left a print, the green gunge had started to burn a hole in the carpet. Reporters from the press, radio, and T V., were having a field day high lighting our particular area as the only infestation of it's kind in the whole of the country. Nowhere else was reported to be experiencing this strange freak of nature. On our tiresome treks to school every morning we were seeing more and more weird and wonderful sights. Car's that had driven over the caterpillars by accident had paid an awful price for their carelessness, as the rubber on their tyres began to bubble up and burn, causing them to deflate because of this mysterious green compound. Also, more alarming news reaching our ears was that some of our friends and their parents, who had been unlucky enough to come into contact with these caterpillars, had received a rash and blisters which had now turned into something more sinister for they were now suffering from severe weight loss and fighting for their very lives. Visiting one of my close friends with my cousin sent the pangs of fear around my body as I gazed at a horror show confronting me. Their body resembled someone being badly burnt in a fire, with huge patches of shiny skin and wide gaping cuts in the skin, visible everywhere.

Danly was protected by wooded slopes and hill's on three sides. We were in fact trapped in a valley. The only access being a narrow strip of land leading to the other numerous mining communities and villages. It was like being in a gigantic sun trap, as the heat generated by the clouded skies increased on a daily basis. Fight's would break out between the rival faction's in our school, sometimes between boys fighting over a girl. One fight I did witness was over a girl called Caron Jarvis. A girl in the class above me. She was a very attractive girl, and boy did she know it. All the boys at school fancied her. Coming back from school one day a fight broke out between two of the boys over Caron, which resulted in one of the boys being pushed into a privet hedge.

Spreading his arms outwards to stop himself, he landed head down on the floor below. Staring down at him he must have crushed some of the caterpillars in his dramatic bid to save himself, and now green gunge was dripping from the branches into his eyes. His scream's of agony could be heard yards away as he frantically tried to remove the substance. Everybody just stood there motionless as we saw the green gunge eating into the flesh on his face and watching in disbelief as his face disintegrated before our very eyes. When the paramedics arrived to render him assistance they were too late. He was dead. Everyone looked at one another astonished it didn't seem possible they were all numb with shock. One minute he was alive the next minute he was dead.

Every morning looking up at those dark unnatural grey cloud's made you wonder what hidden secrets they held. Was someone up there actually staring down at us monitoring our every move?. You always had a strange feeling in the back of your mind of being watched from above. Heat out of all proportion was unbearable as the summer months started. The caterpillar explosion was well and truly out of control, it was affecting everyone in the area. On these hot muggy nights people were leaving their windows wide open to try and let a breathe of fresh air into their homes but was also it an invitation for loosing in unwanted guests. Gossamer and fine net were being sold in the shops at an alarming rate. Even as we slept in our beds at night the caterpillars were climbing in through the open windows and infecting us with the hair on their bodies. More and more cases of this mysterious outbreak was being reported on a daily basis. Uncle Ben was a keen gardener and his garden was his pride and joy. After finishing his shift at the mine, every night he would methodically tend to his plants as though they were his children, weeding out any unwanted items and watering, then feeding the remainder of the vegetables to be dug up later and eaten. His temper got the better of him one night when the sight he saw met his eyes as he walked along the path into the garden. It sent a very mild mannered man into that of a raving lunatic.

"Give me that spade", he shouted out aloud to his wife.

"I'll give then caterpillars what for eating my prize stuff". At that he went charging into the vegetable patch to do battle with the caterpillars. Aunt May followed him and tried to convince him that smashing them with the spade wasn't the answer.

"Okay" he said looking at her with a glint of mischief in his eyes, "let's see how they like fire", he quickly got a fire-can going burning up all the tinder dry garden rubbish he could find. Then getting a stick he began collecting the caterpillars on his spade and started throwing them on the fire. A funny thing happened next. It was unexplainable. As the caterpillars came in contact with the flames, it was like watching a firework going off, as a column of green flame came shooting out of the fire. It only lasted for a couple of seconds then it was all over. When the news of my uncles discovery filtered out bonfires were lit all over the town to combat our new growing menace. Teams of men and women dressed in special white protection suits had been drafted into the area to deal with this abnormal outbreak. Everyone was questioned, young and old alike, to try and get to the bottom of this mysterious phenomena. Cordoning off the whole of the infected area you couldn't get in or out of Danly, bringing our school term to an abrupt end. Strategically placed all over our little town were containers for collecting up these weird looking insects for disposal. This type of experience and actually living through it was a once in a life time event. Now it was being played out before my very eyes. Even our everyday walk to the shops was becoming a risky business, for these furry little monsters were everywhere under your feet. In the trees dropping down on you from above and climbing up the walls in our houses trying to get in. During those few short months the death rate had risen very sharply due to our new intruders.

By some uncanny reason at the start of our new school term in September, all the caterpillars had disappeared. In our science laboratory someone had thoughtfully, as an experiment, had placed six caterpillars in a glass tank with a glass plate on the top. Watching their every move from day to day and writing reports on their habits and progress, watching them eating their way through anything green placed in the tank at a ferocious rate.

We had not been back at school more than a few days monitoring the growth of this strange insect, when we noticed one morning all six had turned to chrysalises. We were waiting for the outcome with baited breath to see what kind of weird and wonderful moths or butterflies they would hatch into. It was a forgone conclusion that whatever they were, would be better than the caterpillars. Our expectations were about to come true. Tuesday morning on our second week at school word was being passed from class to class. The fantasy had at last turned into a reality, for inside the glass tank in our science lab all six had hatched out. All of us had hoped that after all the months of anxiety we would all witness a thing of beauty emerged from the chrysalis, instead they had turned into hideous looking huge mosquito flies.

They had a blood sucking sting in the tail. Large bulging eyes dominated their heads, their transparent bodies and wings resembled the blood veins in your hands. The most frightening thing above all was the aggression shown by them trying to get out and their physical size, being approximately four inches. The mere sight of them when looking into that glass tank turned your blood cold with fright. The local authorities were immediately informed and plans drawn up to deal with our new menace. Now in the bright light of dawn, in our new era came the moment of truth. We had all witnessed the fly hatch in our laboratory fish tank, how many more of these blood sucking parasites were out there?. Complaints were now rolling in blocking up the telephone networks. From all over the area people were being bitten by this strange flying insect. The devastating effects it had confining the infected person to bed immediately which then followed by a fever.

In the case of the caterpillars they were slow moving and so on seeing them you could take the necessary steps to avoid them. Not so with the mosquito flies who were about four inches in length and could blend into the very foundations of our little community. Without any warning they would fly out and attack you. Children swimming in a pond trying to keep cool on a hot day were suddenly attacked without any warning by these blood sucking pests. Another case of an old man and women out walking their pet dog on a warm September's evening were suddenly confronted by a swarm and quickly smothered. A young mother left her baby outside the kitchen window in his pram, takes her eyes off him for a brief instant, only to look back moments later to see the pram full of flying blood sucking insects. New legislation had been passed advising every parent and child to carry a stick with them whenever they went out to swat and kill them . That was the only way to deal with this new infestation pestering everyone, by giving them a good whack. Our very survival was going steadily from bad to worse as more and more deaths were being reported. One of the most bazaar cases I myself having actually experienced was when we were attending the Miner's welfare club on a Saturday night in September. Uncle Ben had flatly refused to let a bunch of flies stop his Saturday night's entertainment. It was eyes down, look in, as the bingo numbers were being called out. The clubs patrons were excitedly marking off their numbers on their tickets to capture that large money prize. Windows and doors had been left wide open to let in the fresh air, it was that hot and clammy you could hardly breathe. Halfway though the night's entertainment a swarm of these strange flying insects flew into the club causing absolute havoc. Beer cans, bottles, and glasses, were thrown at them with devastating affect causing more injuries to their friends than the flies. Ambulances had to be called in to ferry the injured away.

Emergency measures had now been bought into place to deal with the dilemma. The whole area evacuated just like in the war years, spending our lives in temporary accommodation and going by bus to school every morning. Specially trained teams were sent into our little town to deal with and try and control this new menace. Mother nature has her own way of dealing with unwanted elements. Daily hundreds of sea birds were arriving to gobble up this new supply of food. Seeing them darting and diving about in the air catching the large flies in their beaks and digesting them in flight ready for the next one.

Experiments carried out in laboratories up and down the country to try and find out of the origin of the caterpillars and flies all concluded the sad fact the species were unknown. Its body parts and make up was like no other insect on earth. Tests carried out to determine and identify the toxins in their bodies had everyone puzzled it didn't match anything that was known.

Everything about the whole fiasco was just a complete mystery to everyone. It was as though our particular little area had been designated as a test site by something out there in space. Hail stones had born the eggs down to earth where they had laid buried in the soil and germinated by the heat. Then left to their own devices and monitored for the results. Whoever it was, a life form perhaps from another galaxy out there in space trying out an experiment, we shall never know. In my own mind the event in itself was terrifying causing death and carnage in the spate of such a few short months. If the whole saga had been carried out on a larger scale the effects would have been catastrophic. After our return to normality back at my Aunt's house my parents arrived from America to take me back with them. I can remember even to this day the first words out of my fathers mouth. "Have I got something exciting to tell you all".

Uncle Ben nudged me and winked "okay lets hear it, nothing ever exciting happens around here"

That silly reply had me laughing out loud hysterically.

Dad looked at his brother for the answer, only to be told.

"If I tell you the truth you won't believe me".

Now came the biggest surprise of all, mother was expecting her second child which thrilled me to bits, Dad also concluded his talk by inviting Uncle Ben, Aunt May and my two cousins to spend Christmas with them in their new home in America.

Wiping the tears from my eyes with joy on that Christmas holiday sitting down in our new lounge, trying to tell my parents of the strange dilemma we had all experienced, that had only happened a few short months ago. Both looked at me as though I was hallucinating.

Then Uncle Ben leaned over to me" I told you young lady no

one will believe you, to them it's a wild exaggerated story but you and I know different,and that will be our little secret . Standing up he proposed a toast. "To my young brother Rob and his very charming wife. Wishing you both a very merry Christmas and a happy and prosperous new year and good luck with your new venture".

Sarcastically he then remarked "and don't ever spare a thought for me working in the pitch black darkness miles under ground ". Everyone laughed out loud at his comical sense of humour. The truth on a day to day basis has all been recorded in my journal depicting the whole sad saga that happened all those years ago.

THE END

My Old Gang Of Long Ago

Every year on Christmas Eve I carry out my annual ritual of laying a holly wreath with nine small red ribbons tied to it on the branch of an old willow tree. Then I sit back on the wooden bench and reminisce. Behind me our village pond is covered in a thick layer of ice, the suns weak haze glistening off it's surface. A tree that has stood on this spot from the very dawn of time itself looks very much as though it came off a Christmas card with the frost covering it's branches.

Holding back the tears, my memory goes racing back to happier times long ago to our childhood years when we were all young. There were ten of us in our little gang, six boys and four girls and all full of mischief. With the passing of time and after all these years I can still picture their faces in my mind and remember their names. Archie Low was our gang leader, I will never know why, although he was a big lad he wouldn't say boo to a goose. There was Dennis Chapman, if there was trouble brewing you could guarantee it would always manage to find him. Then there were the two brothers, John and Bert Smallman, these two followed Dennis around like shadows. Whenever trouble broke out they used their size and weight to bail him out. Ernie Jones was a shy retiring sort of person, I never knew the attraction in being a member of our gang but he used to stick to us like glue. Ralph Peabody another male member, his father owned the general store in the village, he too was a tall lanky kind of person. Last but not least of the boys was, Gunter Friedman. He was of German origin. His mother had died young so his father sent him to England to be raised by his wife's

English parents, who were, I'm happy to say, my neighbours Fred and Ethel Smart. They owned a small market garden. Now it's the girls turn. First was Valerie Singleton. She was certainly a blonde beauty. Every boy at our school would race to carry her books home from school. Pauline Dickinson was what you might describe as being a big well built girl who could certainly handle herself. You had to watch your p's and q's when she was around or face her wrath. Doreen Samson was like me, average height and weight, she didn't like arguments and would go out of her way to avoid them. Now last of all me, Elizabeth Dawson, Lizzie for short, my father and mother owned a farm at the top of our village only a stone's throw away from where I'm sitting now. Our little gang would meet every school morning under the old willow tree then walk the two miles to school, come rain or shine, and every evening make the long hike back. Times were hard back in those days, but we all stuck together, sharing what we had amongst each other. Images and pictures in my mind remind me of the winter months, having snowball fights and riding on our sledges in the snow and if the village pond froze over, skating on the ice. There was only one problem. We only had one pair of ice skates so we had to take it in turns to use them. Then we watched and laughed as one after the other tumbled and bounced off the ice trying to keep our balance. In the hot dry months of the summer we used to go swimming in a pool in some woods near our farm. There was no such thing as bathing costumes, it was only in the latter years modesty took over. Progressing through our infants stage, then into our teen years we all attended the local college on a variation of different courses. One morning we had the shock of our lives when we heard that Fred and Ethel Smart had died suddenly within hours of one another, and Gunter Friedman had been ordered back to Germany by his father. Standing on that cold drafty railway station in the spring of 1938 and waving goodbye to a dearly beloved friend there wasn't many dry eyes I can tell you. The pictures conjured up in my mind, seeing the train disappearing into the tunnel at the end of the stations platform, and him waving frantically back to us.

Most of us had been pursuing our different studies to try and get our qualifications to better ourselves in life. I was studying farming techniques at the college in the next town.

The next piece of bad news to reach our ears was England had declared war on Germany. From the tone of the broadcasters voice this wasn't going to be an easy war. Members of the gang flocked to volunteer into different branches of the armed forces. Two month's after their enlistment they were allowed some leave before going to their permanent stations. We all met under the branches of this old weeping willow tree. I've never known them look so prim and proper in their new uniforms. It made me feel right out of place having to stay home and manage my parent's farm. Four of the boys had joined the army, one the navy,and the other the RAF, even the girls had joined different branches of the armed forces.

Seeing them all look so smart made me feel envious as I watch them parading about. They all looked so elegant in their brand new uniforms. Doreen had joined the Wrens and she could see me eyeing her up with envy.

"Lizzie" she called to me, "come and try my hat and coat on".

Wearing that hat and coat from that uniform made me feel ten feet tall. It fitted me like a glove, showing off my curvaceous figure to the full. On the day before they all departed I remember Valerie saying to us,

"Wouldn't it be nice if we all left a ribbon on the old willow tree for luck".

Our farm was nearest so I dashed up to the house and got some old red ribbons out of my sewing case. I cut them up into six inch strips, took a hammer and some nails then returned with them back to my friends. Each of us then in turn drove a nail into the old tree and tied a piece of ribbon to it. Making a solemn gang vow that after the conflict was over we would all return home and retrieve our ribbons off the nails from the old willow tree. That was the last time we were all alive as a gang . Picture postcards send to me by my friends of their different locations made me feel envious and wish I was there. We kept in touch by writing, some had been posted oversea's, and it was nice to get the occasional post card showing an exotic scene. During my years spent at college, taking my degree in farming and agriculture. I had met and fallen in love with a young man named David. He to was a farmer. We got married in the spring of 1940 and twelve months later I delivered a bonny bouncing girl. We got some group pictures developed of my husband, baby girl and myself and sent it to all my friends reminding them all they were the child's godparents.

News on the radio was going from bad to worse with our ships being sunk daily. Then the army's evacuation from Dunkirk leaving a lot of our boys behind on the beaches. On our farm I was comparatively safe locked away in the country side, but my friends were feeling the brunt of the Nazi invasion. Mishaps and disasters were the thing of the day with our tiny island home now under the threat of invasion. Every Sunday morning attending our local church with my daughter and mother gave me the opportunity to talk to my friends parents. This particular Sunday I could feel that sense of sorrow filling the air. Listening to our local preacher rounding off his sermon by saying, heart felt condolences for the loss of their respective daughters,Pauline, and Valerie, who had been killed in an air raid in London on the Friday night of that week. Those few words from that sermon seemed to bounce about my brain. I just couldn't take it in. Only a few months ago we were all talking about making plans for the future. Now two of the girls were dead. Returning home from church my whole body seemed paralysed with the sad news. Sitting down on a chair I cried like a baby. My brain could not absorb it . Like a thunder bolt out of the blue my husband dropped another bombshell. He had been called up to join the army and had to report for duty at the end of the week. The feeling that came over me as I stared at him was unexplainable. It was like someone walking over my grave .

Ernie Jones, had joined the navy and while out shopping with my daughter in our town one summer's morning his mother came up to me with tear filled eyes and told me his ship had been torpedoed and there were no survivors. Ralph Peabody would send me the occasional letter. I was horrified to learn that he had been taken prisoner and later a letter was sent to me by one of his friends saying he had died in the winter of 1942 in captivity from pneumonia. Doreen Samson had been stationed in Gibraltar also used to correspond with me on a regular basis but by the sound of her last letter all was not well. She had picked up a life threatening virus.

Archie, now the proud owner of a green beret was in the commandos. While visiting his parents recently, I was told he had been killed in action on the D-day landings. My nerves were in shreds at that piece of news, all my friends that I had grown up with had died one way or another in this terrible war.

Of the other three a black edged telegram shown to me by one of their parents simply read, 'Missing believed lost.!' In those war torn years of uncertainty, friends from my childhood had all died very young fighting for their country. Sitting on the old wooden bench under the willow tree I swore a vow there and then that every Christmas eve as long as I lived a holly wreath would be placed on a branch of the old willow tree in remembrance of my old gang who had perished in the war.

Their ribbons now tattered and faded still hang proudly on the nails we placed there all those many years ago.To my utter surprise in the autumn of 1945 David, my husband looking a bit worse for wear came walking through the door. He had at least survived the war, after his return to civy street I bore him two more children. Two beautiful boys.

Holding this holly wreath in my hands on this cold December day, has sent my mind racing back in time. Of the ten in the gang I am the only one who has retrieved her ribbon. Good luck has smiled on me over the passing years. Having my children and now my grandchildren, for I have now reached the ripe old age of sixty achieving all my goals in life. All my three children are doing well. My eldest daughter has a family of her own and it won't be long before the two boys fly the coup.

We all made our plans for the future all those many years ago but due to the circumstances of war. I'm afraid it will never happen.

A sixth sense told me that I was not alone but being watched. Someone's eyes were penetrating the back of my neck. Turning around slowly, facing me was a middle aged man, wearing a thick dark brown overcoat and trilby hat with a young girl at his side.

"Excuse me", he said in a very polite accent, "I'm looking for.... a Miss Lizzie Dawson".

Looking at him in bewilderment I answered him back, "That is I".

"Forgive me I'm forgetting my manners" he said. "Gunter Freidman was my late father, I am his only son Hans. His last wish on his deathbed in 1946 he made me swear on oath. That I was to return to England and retrieve his ribbon and meet with you and tell you the events leading up to his death". He and his daughter sat down beside me on that old wooden bench and began telling me his astonishing story. Which I might say in all honesty took all the wind out of my sails.

He began.

My father after leaving England in 1938 got himself a job in Germany as a security guard at the bank in our town on the French German border. Over the next few years the might of the German war machine needed more men so he was drafted into the army and soon became an officer. After the D day landings in June 1944 the allied advance was like a huge conveyor belt overrunning German held positions. In the aftermath of the advance my father was captured. An officer sent to interrogate him was none other than Dennis his old school friend from England. Over the next few hours while Dennis was interrogating my father he kept going back to his job at the bank. It was as though the word bank had taken precedence over everything. On his third visit to see him he took my father completely by surprise when he outlined his plan to rob the bank, which my father refused point blank to do. But Dennis had a very persuasive and manipulative attitude and he soon convinced my father of all the advantages, pointing out to him the bank had been partly destroyed in an air raid and was now in allied hands. The task could be undertaken and carried out with the minimum of risk making all concerned very rich. Dennis explained in detail to my father that with all the fighting going on above ground nobody would bat an eyelid to what was happening under their very feet. Filling out the appropriate forms he ensured my fathers release into his custody. Now came the pain-staking task of working out a plan to get into the bank vault below ground without being seen, because the battle outside the town would not last forever. During my fathers employment at the bank he mentioned the fact that building contractors had been called in to lay a new sewage pipe from the basement into the main sewer tunnel. All work had been carried out underground. Stored in the basement were the main bank vaults holding deposit boxes containing valuable items. Dennis was like somebody who had just found a pot of gold at the end of the rainbow. As he and my father took, bearings and map references   the bank now lay under a pile of rubble due to the constant bombardment. One day out reconnoitering the area they came across a bombed out factory and to their surprise a crater had been formed by a bomb blast. Looking down the hole they could see a tunnel. Investigating it more thoroughly it was the main sewer tunnel leading into the town. Dennis was so excited at his new find he took a torch out of the jeep he was driving and climbed down the hole to investigate it further. All their dreams and expectations were coming true. The sewer tunnel led right up the main high street, past the bank, also he could see where the contractors had installed the new pipe from the basement. To carry out an operation of this kind needed more labour. Two of Dennis's old school pals the Smallman brothers were recruited. Both had knowledge of explosives. A further four were recruited to help dig their way to the bank vault wall because time was of the essence.

Dennis's jeep had been parked inside the bombed out factory building. The work progressing well. They were now on the last leg of their task to blast a way into the bank through the wall. As the seven of them came out of the hole and made their way to the jeep they started unloading the explosives. Suddenly they came under a hail of machine gun fire from a German infantry patrol. My father was hit twice and lay along-side the jeeps wheels. Dennis and the two Smallman brothers dashed out of the cover and started to drag my father by his hands clear of the jeep in case a stray bullet hit the explosives, all he can remember was an almighty bang.

One morning to my surprise the police came to my home and said my father was alive and in a military hospital. The year was 1946. This came as rather a shock because I was given the impression he had been killed in action defending the town. Over the next few weeks and months visiting him on a regular basis was when all the jigsaw parts were put together and he unravelled this incredible story making me promise on his last dying breath that I should return to England one day in the future and look you up. I was also to take over my grandfathers small holding. However due to hardships suffered after the end of the war. It's taken me a long time to achieve this ambition but a promise is a promise.'

Looking at Hans you could see his fathers determination in his eyes. Pointing to the old willow tree, "up there is part of our history there are ten nails one for every member of our gang we made a vow that whoever survived the war should retrieve his or her ribbon, I'm afraid I'm the only survivor".

Pointing at the pool behind the willow tree, "many years ago on a very cold winter's day when we were all young we were playing on the pond. Dare-devil Dennis as usual was showing off when the ice suddenly broke plunging him and Bert Smallman into that cold icy water. Gunter your father as quick as a flash leapt onto the ice spread eagleing his body, while John Smallman held his legs, as he plunged his top half under the water to find Dennis and Bert. They were both wearing scarves so your dad grabbed the scarves and pulled them both up from the icy depths to safety. During the war years I've spent many lonely hours on this bench dreaming of home comings and happy reunions, the whole gang returning home victorious from the conflict. Starting up their own families, parties for the children and grandchildren,. It's all just an old woman's dream it will never happen".

Hans tapped Lizzie on the arm, " Its never too late you know. Now I've seen the old place I can go back to Germany and collect my wife and my younger children and we can make the old place come back to life once again".

THE END

ORCHIDS OF THE MOON

There was a clanking and grinding of the key in the lock engaging the tumblers as the prison guard opened the huge steel door. The loud deafening bang as it closed behind me sending that sudden rush of air around my body... And....Oh ! the sweet smelling taste of free fresh air, it was like stepping into another world. After serving six years of my life in that hell hole called prison. Through my long confinement being cooped up in a prison cell, during those dark days of despair, never once did I moan and groan but got on with the tasks allotted to me. Being a model prisoner my hard work, efforts, and good conduct and due to extenuating circumstances beyond my control. Fresh evidence in my case had been received by the authorities and investigated, granting me an early parole, so I could try and piece my shattered life together once again. I'm not one of life's habitual criminals, neither, thief, robber or a killer but one of societies unsung hero's. Jennifer Anabel Soammes is my name and my only crime to society was being in the wrong place at the wrong time. Six years is like an eternity when you have nothing better to do with your time than watch the paint dry on the walls and see the spiders weave their webs. Sometimes counting my lucky stars I've survived this long in that environment for I shall be fifty five in ten days time. But the most important date on the yearly calender was my forthcoming marriage to my second husband just two weeks before Christmas. Although I say so myself and if I'm allowed to blow my own trumpet, I'm not bad looking for a woman of my years, doing plenty of daily exercise while in prison, has kept my figure well proportioned and in trim. One thing that has been constantly on my mind after my release was finalised, was to visit my two grown up daughters who are both married and see my new grandchildren.

Looking back in disbelief at those foreboding doors of steel reminded me of the tragic events leading to me serving six years of my life in there. Even now thinking about it, the thought, sends a cold shiver right down my spine. All those miserable years of my life spent in captivity will remain embedded in my mind for the remainder of my life on this earth. Though at least , I have the satisfaction in my own mind, that my untimely act, leading to my arrest has rid humanity of a serious threat to its very existence. Although the sentence metered out to me was for the punishment that fitted the crime I have no remorse on that score.   Like any tale of woe, true or false, nobody wants to believe them. Family ties with the church have always held a strong conviction for me, giving me the courage strength and faith to carry out my aspirations to the bitter end, and as sure as God is my judge every event that has happened in my life over the last eight years is true.

It all started one bright and sunny spring morning, when the love of my life, my husband Alec, walked out on me and my children never to return. I've turned this matter over and over in my mind trying to find a reason why and for the life of me there's just no answer. Born with a silver spoon in one's mouth gets you off to a good start in life. Where nothing was too expensive, best schools, good education, lots of rich friends and a good career. During my teenage years, certain times in the yearly calender, balls were arranged so that young unattached females could meet all the eligible bachelors, and that's how I met my now late husband   Alec, at a summer ball.   Where I must say in all honesty, it was love at first sight. He was tall and good looking and reminded me of a knight of old in shining armour who came charging down and completely swept me off my feet.. He came from a wealthy family with a good career in front of him, you might say any starry eyed girls dream man. Eighteen months later we tied the knot and got married. I have two adorable daughters from the marriage.

Everything went bottoms up and turned sour one spring morning sending all my hopes and dreams for the future crashing down around my head. Discovering to my heart-ache that my perfect man had walked out on me and our children for a younger model. This whole sad turn of events had a devastating effect on my life and left me heart broken. With my married life in ruins all my plans for the future had suddenly come to an abrupt end. After spending my life, being waited on, hand and foot, and having everything done for me, I was now confronted with the daunting prospects of bringing up my two children alone. One good thing about the whole sad affair was my late parents had left me well provided for, and the house we lived in had been bought by my parents as a wedding gift. So at least I had a roof over my head.

Now came a bitter blow to my system, you might say the turning point in my lavish life style. Up to this moment in time, life had been one happy go lucky merry-go- round, having all my worries about household bills disregarded as Alec took care of those. 'Now', came the turning point in my life and the events that would introduce me to the other side of the coin, and send me down the slippery slope of despair and finally my confinement in prison for six years. Thinking about this whole sad saga, its even stranger than fiction itself. it seems impossible to be true but I'll swear this on my mothers grave every actuality did happen.

Eight years ago I was out celebrating my forty seventh birthday, a divorcee with two teenage girls looking for husband number two. Even in the blackest of days I have always taken a pride in my appearance, keeping my figure in trim and making myself attractive and presentable. Long blond hair being one of my many attributes which was cut in the bob fashion, a nice pleasant smile and bubbling personality. So I decided to chance my luck and put myself back on the market and see what turned up.

A group of my very close well meaning friends decided to drag me out of my doldrums and the world of self pity by indulging ourselves in a night out to remember. First a meal at a fashionable restaurant, followed by an exciting talk by a very famous explorer, Professor Frederick Egan at our local village hall. Thinking back now to the event it was all a very moving experience in my life at the time.

By using still slides from a film projector Professor Egan was able to explain in great detail the topics on each slide. As he rambled on telling us stories of his many explorations, the whole subject in itself was breath-taking, as, I might add so too was the lecturer. He was a very handsome looking man with the most striking pair of blue eyes I had ever seen. Finding myself totally spellbound by his appearance, it seemed as though his eyes were transfixed on me as I found myself clinging on to his every word. After a very enlightening and descriptive talk we were shown some of his artifacts that he had collected over the years on his many journeys of discovery around the world. Browsing around one piece in particular caught my eye and aroused my imagination holding me like a magnet. It was an old brown parchment painting of a group of Black Orchids in a jungle clearing. Standing there mesmerised by the sheer beauty of the picture in front of me, my whole body was trembling and shuddering with excitement, I failed to noticed mine host standing right behind me viewing my every move with curiosity.

"Can I be of any service,..... that old parchment painting you have been admiring dates back hundreds of years,..... It's Jennifer isn't it,?" he had a lovely captivating smile as he spoke to me, the kind that can drive a woman wild with desire.

Smiling straight back at him I replied "Yes that's certainly my name, and indeed you can", pointing at the black orchids in the old parchment painting ...." those black flowers."? Before having time to finish my sentence he butted in my conversation.

"Those black flowers as you aptly put it" .he than began explaining the plants origins.... "Were the most deadliest and dangerous plants that had ever grown on this planet . No one knows where they came from, or how they came to be here, but there's one thing certain for sure, they certainly didn't come from this world ".

"Many years spent on dangerous journeys of discovery studying and researching the origins of this mythical plant has taken me all over back waters of the Amazon jungle. Collecting scraps of information here and there. Some fact, some fiction and some based on old legends and some on old wives tales.

With all the information I have amassed about this particular period I can safely say around the year 1700 even the dates are based on hear-say. Deep in the jungles of the Amazon rain forests a tribe of Indians worshipped these Moon Orchids, to them they were like gods. Information received from various sources said the plants could converse with them telepathically and give them instructions on how to improve their daily lives. They were like no other plants on this earth. Standing over ten feet tall with a large black flowering orchid as big as a football on a stout single stem. Dominating the whole plant, it must have been an awesome sight indeed. Normally plants go through the various cycles in their growth, some die off in winter, then start growing again in spring, some shed all their leaves and petals then start the whole cycle over again. Like wise some flower in winter some in spring,summer, autumn . Information gathered about these Moon Orchids said they never died. It was as though they were ever lasting, regenerating their specie by sending out suckers to start up another plant.

According to myths and superstitious legends passed down from generation to generation and told to me, about the, Moon Orchids, or Orchids of the Moon as they were called. It was a name given to them by the Indians. This all started one day when a recently married south American Indian man and woman were collecting wood in the forest. Suddenly in the jungle clearing a huge black orchid manifested itself before their very eyes, Both of them on seeing this strange phenomena were paralysed with fear. Feeling a strange sensation in their minds, it appeared to give them instructions. It told them of a girl child the woman would soon give birth to, and that she would be like no other in her tribe. Her skin would be white like the driven snow, and her name must be Evalanti. The voice continued saying Evalanti would grow up into a mighty Queen bringing wisdom and leadership to her tribe and they would flourish and prosper beyond any one's wildest dreams.

A vision of enchantment seen in a jungle clearing to the mind of a poor Indian woman, now the first part of prophesy was coming true. A child was born to her not dark skinned like her parents and tribe, but white like the driven snow just as the moon orchid had predicted. Evalanti grew at an alarming rate she was a very beautiful maiden, tall and stout of limb,and as strong and fearless as the lion.

Legend goes on to say, to stare into the beautiful bewitching face of Evalanti was an experience in itself. Her soft brown hazel eyes shone like an erupting fiery volcano. Jet black long straight hair hung down her back. She was born not like any other but to be a warrior and leader of her people. Her limbs were straight and strong like the mighty oak tree.

On Evalanti's thirteenth birthday her mother took her into the forest as instructed, to meet the strange Moon Orchid on the night of the golden moon. Standing there proud and naked but for a skimpy loin cloth clinging to her well formed hips, she was now six feet tall dwarfing her mother. Evalanti could hear words being imprinted on her brain as the Moon Orchid began giving her instructions.

'You have pleased me very much with your progress and have blossomed out into a fine young female warrior. Now with my help and guidance you will become a mighty Queen and your domain will be boundless. As for me in return for my wisdom, my reproductive organs are now sending out suckers to enable my specie to grow, flourish, and multiply even beyond your wildest dreams. To help me in this reproduction process a constant supply of fresh meat is needed every full moon. Namely captives from other tribes. Men, women, and children must be sacrificed.to feed me. Instructions will be given to you on their preparation and the amount for incarceration. Now go out this day and select yourself fifty warriors both men and women from outlying tribes and bring them to me by the next full moon. The chosen one's will be initiated by drinking the sap from my roots then given the divine right to serve me for the rest of their days and I will make them feared and respected amongst the bravest of men. Is that understood Evalanti ?'

She nodded her head in agreement.

'Your tribe has been chosen by me for one special purpose. You have been down trodden for years and laughed at, and your lands and live stock stolen, forcing you to live a miserable existence and a life of poverty in this remote delta region on the mighty Amazon river. From this day forth the name of Evalanti will bring fear to the hearts of even the bravest of men. After my inspection and initiation of your followers, your first target will be the lands to the North. These must be conquered and overrun captives must be taken, men, women and children brought before me here, is that understood ?'. Evalanti again nodded her head.

Their first mission set out by the Moon Orchid was to be an arduous one as the Northern tribes were known to be very strong and powerful and had many warriors. Evalanti and her band of fifty followers both male and female were nearing one of the northern tribes larger villages. Suddenly they were surrounded by scores of painted tribesmen all yelling and whooping brandishing spears.

At once on seeing Evalanti, their chief indicated to his men he wanted the half naked white girl brought before him. Two of the tribesmen rushed out from the ranks and seized Evalanti and held her by the arms. With a rush of almighty supernatural power she picked up both and bodily swung them around like rag dolls smashing their heads to pulp in the process. Two more were sent to restrain her, they too suffered the same fate, then two more. and so on, and so on until their were a heap of dead bodies in a mound, all meeting with the same gruesome fate.

This strange turn of events frightened the tribal chief into believing Evalanti was some kind of goddess sent to rule over them and she was here to teach them a lesson. Lifting up his arms he began bowing in front of his new mistress. As he listened to her terms of surrender which meant captives being sent to the Moon Orchids as well as valuable items. This type of harrowing story was being repeated time and time again over the next twenty five years and her raids became more daring frequent and gruesome. Anyone who stood against her faced a fate worse than death. Where once stood a small village of mud huts in the jungle, a settlement made out of stone had suddenly sprung up from the very swamp lands it had once occupied. Brick built houses, streets paved with stone and a huge palace had been built for their beloved Queen, Evalanti. In the jungle clearing where the Moon Orchids grew a high stone wall had been built around them for protection. Their numbers had now increased to eighty, and still more land was being cleared and fresh Corms sown to produce even more. It's design had been carefully thought out. Only one entrance through a small tunnel into the forbidden compound, and once in, there was no escape. Over the years the Moon orchids appetite for fresh human meat was inexhaustible. Every month with the big full moon shining out of a dark blue sky Evalanti and her tribe would celebrate the occasion by feasting and wild dancing. On the stroke of midnight the gates to the tunnel would be opened and the poor unsuspecting captives driven inside. It was said their pathetic screams could be heard all night and as many as thirty or forty a time were sacrificed to them. Evalanti's small army were under tremendous strain and even they were finding it hard to please their new masters venturing into unknown territories to get even more captives

One bright sacrificial moonlight night, a male captive managed to escape over the compound wall and decided to see what happened to his fellow captives. After climbing back up the wall from the other side, the sight below him sickened his stomach at the carnage being carried out below. Poor helpless captives, men, women, and children, were left wondering about inside facing these strange looking flowers. Their root like tentacles were stretching out all over the floor. To step on one meant instant death for it immediately wrapped itself around its prey. Depending on how many tentacles from the different orchids had caught their unsuspecting victims, it usually ended up in a tug of war literally ripping their poor bodies apart. Then the morsels left were dragged inside the base of their roots to be digested. Screaming was of no avail for there was no one to there to listen. Watching the whole inhuman gruesome spectacle sickened him so much at the scene in front of him. He immediately clambered down and braving the dangers of the jungle walked hundreds of miles to the nearest European outpost and told them his sickening story. Soldiers were immediately dispatched with guns and gunpowder to destroy Evalanti's army and the orchids. Primitive weapons were no match for artillery and gunpowder and the tribe were soon defeated and all the plants burnt and destroyed. Only a few survived the massacre by fleeing and hiding in the jungle Evalanti being one of them and they haven't been seen since.

Hearing the professor's strange tale had a devastating effect on me psychologically.

For in response all of my nerves seemed to be shaking,....... "And you say.... this Queen Evalanti and the Moon orchids have never been seen right up to this very day. Suddenly a rush of blood to my head sent everything black sending me collapsing onto the floor. All I can remember next was my friends all fussing around me trying to revive me. Professor Frederick Egan a fine charming gentleman also played his part in trying to resuscitate me by giving me smelling salts. Looking back at that particular incident still brings a smile to my face,for his comments amused me.

"Some of my talks can be a bit boring, being applauded by boo's or jeers, but I have never known anyone faint before. His hand then began stroking my forehead which immediately had a arousing effect on me awakening me from my slumber.

Then I began telling him the reason for my lapse into unconsciousness. "You say those Moon orchids haven't been seen since Evalanti's defeat hundreds of years ago?".

"That is quite true" Professor Egan replied.

'Well I've got some bad news for you Professor, for there are twenty of them growing in my step mother's conservatory, plus the fact Carla my stepmother could easily pass as your mythical Queen Evalanti "

This bombshell and sudden outburst stopped the professor dead in his tracks.

"But that's impossible", he blurted out, "research into this project has taken years to compile. There is no known specie of this orchid on this entire planet. Its a mere superstitious myth. If you believe in a world of fantasy tales, or science fiction, these particular plants probably came from out there in space and landed in the Amazon rain forests, took root and started to grow.? Vague reports made out at the time indicating that a thorough search was made of the whole area looking after all the plants which were burnt and destroyed. There was no indication after a complete investigation ever linked to the Moon orchids being man eaters, so it was dismissed as pure superstitious nonsense. From statements taken from some of the surviving villagers, records showed that when questioned, thousands of poor souls, men, women, and children were sacrificed to these meat eating flowers however there was never any proof to back it up. Old weather beaten parchment paintings found at the scene which had survived the sands of time, showed crude drawings. The orchids were described as being jet black in colour, standing well over ten feet tall, and the actual flower as big as a football. They also had long pointed razor sharp leaves coming up from the base of the plant, and a complex rooting system which spread it's tentacles over the floor to catch its prey.

No Jennifer I would definitely say your mistaken."

His last comment made me furious and caused me to sit up and take note and categorically in no uncertain terms told him, ..."Those plants you have just described to me are growing at this very moment in my stepmother's very large conservatory, and this I will Swear to on the Holy bible".

"To stop any argument I will tell you the whole story of how these so called Moon orchids happen to be in our conservatory. On my twenty fourth birthday my husband Alec and I were married. Six months later both of my parents went on a vacation for twelve months to the Amazon rain forests in Brazil. Mom and Dad were very keen collectors of rare and exotic orchids having a large conservatory to house them at home. Returning back to England in the spring of the following year, they were ecstatic at their unusual find for they bought back with them twenty small rare orchid plants in large wooden cases. They also bought soil and jungle foliage from the area they were discovered in which to grow them in. The biggest surprise of all was a women came to care and nurture them. She indeed was a surprise in itself standing nearly six feet tall with jet black hair, very shapely and, very, attractive. Their new find caused so much excitement in the orchid world that work was started : Immediately demolishing the old conservatory, and constructing another on the same site. It was a very large conservatory to house these new plants in, I'll endorse the word large, it was colossal. Living only ten miles away from my father and mother, visits to them were frequent usually once a week.

My mother had a good well developed body but to my utter despair on my visits I couldn't help but notice she was slowly going to skin and bones. This alarmed me so much that an appointment was made for her immediately at our local hospital. Here she could see a specialist, tests were carried out, and I was given the heart rendering news that my mother had only weeks to live.

All of their married lives my father and mother were a devoted couple. They shared everything together, and at her death my father was devastated. He looked as though his whole world had collapsed and come to an abrupt end. It was nothing to see him talking to himself as he walked around the house in a daze. When I spoke to him he hardly recognised my voice. The situation was getting intolerable so I decided to rearrange my work schedules to make it possible to visit him more often. (Plus the fact) I was also the proud mother of a bonny little bouncing girl Jane, whown my father idolised which may help him with his grief.

The passing of time Like the blinking of an eye. Two more years of my life had flashed by, and on one of my many visits to see my Dad he broke the alarming news to me that he intended marrying Carla, the women they had bought back with them from Brazil. At that moment in time that piece of news sent the shock waves bouncing around my body and I told him so in no uncertain terms. This arrangement was unacceptable, but what

92

could I do?.

Jane my little daughter used to take great delight in going into the conservatory to see all her grandads pretty flowers, especially those rare black orchids they had bought back from Brazil. Their mere size would overwhelm her as she gazed up at them. Some in flower were at least ten feet tall with big black flowers as big as footballs on the end of a long thick stout stem, surrounded by a large base of long razor sharp pointed leaves. Emerging from it and straddling across the floor was a strange network of tentacle shaped roots. You know, it might sound silly now, but walking with my daughter in that conservatory made me feel funny and gave me a haunting sensation as though the orchids were inside my mind and undressing me garment by garment. It all sounds preposterous but at the time it wasn't funny. They were by far one the weirdest flowers I had ever encountered and the very sight of them was enough to give you nightmares. Walking through that conservatory and stepping over their roots strewn all over the floor, was a frightening experience, imagining that at any moment they were going to seize me with their tentacles and wrap them around my body and devour me. I complained bitterly on numerous occasions to my father of the possible dangers. My main concern was my small daughter in case she wandered into the conservatory by accident and the orchids could do her a great deal of harm. As usual Carla, now my ever knowing stepmother reassured me that the plants were harmless but to stop any likely-hood of an accident occurring, a lock would be fitted to a strong door on the conservatory to stop any accidental access.

With the passing of time another addition had been added to my family, my youngest daughter Beth. To my utter surprise Carla was the perfect grandma she would spoil the two youngsters rotten, she had her own way of talking, and amusing them, which the children loved. It was nothing to see her frolicking about on the floor with the two youngsters on top of her for she had boundless energy.

Visiting my father on a regular basis his attitude towards my family was starting to get very hostile, as though he didn't even want us to be there. This in turn spilled over and caused problems in my own family. As usual my ever knowing step mother had all the answers,

"You have caught him on a bad day'. she would remark then start laughing.

His whole behaviour pattern had changed dramatically in just a few short months, it was as though when we were in conversation together his thoughts were being controlled telepathically by something else. He had always been an excellent speaker and could converse on any subject. This strange turn of events really put the strain on our marriage, feeling myself getting very snappy and irritable at the slightest thing. and that isn't me. It wasn't long after that a shock telephone call came one morning in late September, Carla gave me the heart breaking news that my Father had received a massive stroke and died.

After my fathers funeral visits to see my step mother were now on a monthly basis. She had been bequeathed half the house in settlement of my father's will, but the other half belonged to me as part of a legacy handed down by my late grandmother. One particular occasion and on a rare unscheduled visit, I noticed she was taking a lot of interest in my husband, Alec, and he in she. After we left he was challenged about his flirting with my step mother, only to be told that I was imagining things.

Jane and Beth were now teenagers, and took a huge delight in going into the conservatory to see the giant orchids. They were fascinated by the sheer size of them, all twenty orchids were now in full flower and making a breath-taking spectacle to be behold. They were enormous,and well over ten feet tall.

Professor Egan his face now deadly serious butted into Jennifer story once again, "And you say these orchids are growing at your late father's house in the conservatory.?"

" Yes" I replied, " but wait there's more. On one of my visits to see my step mother my two girls used to love to go and see her, they were mesmerised with Carla's wild antics and she certainly knew how to keep them amused. Mrs Phillips my late father's housekeeper, and the cook, had been replaced by all new much younger members of staff, in fact, there seemed to be more staff in the house than it needed. Even more stranger then fiction on every visit to see her, there seemed like a constant supply of new faces appearing from out of nowhere. When questioning my step mother on this subject, she simply said," you can't seem to keep the staff these days". Two much older men were relaying Carla's orders to her staff, one acted as a cook, the other a body-guard over the conservatory, and they were always there eyeing me up.

Now came another body blow in my life, my husband Alec left me, for what I was told to live with a much younger woman. This came as a bitter blow to my system. Outwardly, my marriage had been built on a good foundation which I thought would last to the end of our lives. When my step mother heard from me of his leaving, she coldly said, 'you're better off without him, there's other fish in the sea".

Also on my visits to see her I couldn't help but notice the way she treated her staff. They were little more than slaves, instead of employees. Passing them by if they didn't bow their heads in respect her body-guard would soon tear them of a strip. The whole situation seemed very strange to me. Another dramatic change in her character was when she was married to my father she had always chosen to wear long dresses down to her ankles with plenty of padding underneath and a head scarf. This had now all gone and was replaced by a tall very beautiful woman, with jet black hair which she let fall loosely over her shoulders. Alluring brown hazel eyes that could drive a man wild with desire, and a very curvaceous figure that any younger woman would be envious of. The grey European two piece costume she wore moulded to the contours of her body like a well fitting glove. Another point I couldn't get my mind around was the length of her skirts had also changed dramatically choosing to have the hem line two inches above the knee showing off a pair of very shapely legs. The transformation troubled me at the time as my step mother had to be in her middle sixties if she were a day low and behold before me stood a much younger woman.

95

Once again the Professor interrupted my story,

" Jennifer would it be possible to visit your step mother's home because what you have just told me, means we could all be in great danger. Those enormous black orchids are carnivorous and will only eat human meat according to my research on this subject, that would account for the large number of staff at your late father's house. In the old parchment documents, which have furnished me with a great deal of knowledge about this particular period, as many as thirty a time were sacrificed to the Moon Orchids on the night of the golden moon for they had an usual large appetite.

His philosophies were beginning to worry me, "As a matter of fact' I answered," I'm taking my two daughters with their respective boyfriends, down to see her two weeks on Saturday, that's midsummers night. We have been invited to a fancy dress party, as the wording put's it to celebrate the Lunar festival of the Golden Moon. It's an open invitation for me to bring a friend, you can come down with me then and see for yourself if you wish. However I must emphasise the fact you must wear fancy dress from the early Latin American Indian era."

"Oh that's no problem" he said graciously bowing his head, and thank you for your kind invitation".

On our arrival at my step mother's by mini bus on the night of the party,we had all taken our costumes to heart, even the wearing of war paint to make us all look authentic. Beth was a wizard on the sewing machine so she had made and designed the costumes for the three girls from photographs from the period choosing bolero type blouses with rows of large pretty coloured beads around our necks and very short mini skirts indeed, showing off our legs to the full. She had also used her expertise and chosen for the men skin type trousers with skin type waist-coats covered in coloured beads leaving their arms bare. Looking back now I was a bit apprehensive wondering whether the professor would wear his costume but he had no qualms about it and took it all in good fun.

Carla, well, when she throws a party certainly goes to no expense, exotic plants of all sizes and shapes decorated the large entrance hallway. The whole of the downstairs part of the house had been transformed into a jungle to depict the period and atmosphere. During the years I had seen lavish parties held here but never one like this. Both my mother and father came from weathly families so when they wed had purchased this very large house in it's own grounds. A long drive with trees on both sides led up to a large spacious car park leading to the main entrance hall with its square shaped open staircase leading off to the various bedrooms. Getting into the house was an experience in itself for two huge men dressed in feather head-dresses and feather skirts brandishing spears guarded the entrance, demanding our invitation cards before entry. Carla's popularity became very evident on the amount of guests and close friends who had travelled from around the world to celebrate this special occasion, being of all creeds and nationalities they seemed a weird bunch. It reminded me of a witches coven you read about in fairy tale books. There must have been about sixty in all and some of their costumes take some believing. One south American man wore a very small lion cloth his body painted in black and red strips and a feathered head dress. His wife, or girl friend, if you could call what she wore a costume it was simply strings of beads hanging from various parts of her body to hide her vital parts.

The old house had a large back lawn which Carla had also taken advantage of by staging every conceivable game to enable the guests to mingle and get to know each other. They arranged from games with bat and ball, to leap frog, archery, and spear throwing at targets where all the men were showing off their prowess to their female partners. Fred and the two boys all were doing their fair share of flexing their muscles to impress their lady loves. The games on the lawn finally finished at 7..30 with a tug of war were both males and females joined in the activity,all perspiring on this hot humid night in that warm still air not even a breeze blew. Everyone was now making their way back inside the house to enjoy the rest of the night's entertainment and delights. People I had never seen before in my life were coming up to me and introducing themselves. My poor rear end was covered in bruises after being slapped and pinched by over excited friends of Carla's. Honesty I felt like the Christmas turkey being prodded and patted before being put in the oven to cook. To accommodate seating arrangements for her many guests, double doors on the main big rooms had been left wide open to stop anyone feeling isolated. Doors on the conservatory with a three foot barrier across were also left wide open to give you a panoramic view of the plants inside. Freds face was like wax as he stared at the huge moon orchids dominating the whole scene, moonlight being the only light in the room giving them an unnatural incandescent glow, even in that atmosphere the mere sight of them sent shivers down my spine. Electric lighting for the night had been turned off, leaving the flickering flames from a vast amount of pretty coloured candles to illuminate the rooms. Tables covered in bright exotic orchids had been laid out and placed in strategic points in rooms leading off from the main hallway with all the fruits you could mention plus rare and exotic delicacies. Young boys and girls naked but for a small loin cloth were administering to your every whim. Strange cocktails and food was being serve to you as though it had gone out of fashion The six of us sat at a table in the hallway facing what looked like a small dance floor in front of the conservatory doors. When two hands were placed over my eyes, and a soft voice whispered in my ear, "those skimpy costumes have bought out the savage in you". Releasing her grip, and blinking my eyes to focus on her, the sight in front of me made me rub my eyes with disbelief. When I say strings of beads, for that was all she was wearing, some hanging down from her neck to cover her well formed breasts the others hanging down from her waist to cover her curvaceous thighs. Fred's first reaction at meeting Carla, well he just stood there dumbstruck looking as though he had been hypnotised.

She broke his trance by taking him by the hand. "and who might this handsome young man be?".

"Carla may I introduce my escort, Professor Fred Egan who has been dying to see your Moon Orchids'.

"I hope the wait was worth while. For they have now reached maturity and need to be fed now on a regular basis" smiling she

After a delicious meal served to us by our half naked waiters and waitresses, some of the guests changed into strange looking tribal costumes. Then they then began entertaining us with old tribal music, songs, dances and limbo dances, to commemorate the different seasons of the year. They invited the energetic people there present to join in the limbo dancing, swaying our bodies in time with the music, we negotiated the poles as they were lowered. Each being eliminated one by one. The last two left standing to my surprise were Beth and Carla both goading each other to go lower. Haunting music played on strange looking flutes echoed through the walls of the old house. This had a very embracing and entertaining effect on me making me feel all warm inside. Then came the high-light of the night as the clock struck twelve followed by a drum roll. One of Carla's male guests made an announcement and introduced Carla and two more female guests who were about to entertain us with a dance to celebrate the midsummers full moon. All three painted with tribal markings were completely naked except for a very flimsy G string, dancing with spears their erotic poses and gestures left very little to the imagination. As the dance reached fever pitch all the guests were chanting and tapping their tables keeping in tune with the dancer's movements. Their eyes focused on Carla's beautiful frame as she swayed and contoured her body in sexual gestures. Three young boys and girls walked slowly forward all were naked carrying a small bowl from which Carla reached in with her fingers marking each one in turn with strange markings on their bodies. They followed as mindless souls as Carla and the dancers led them into the conservatory the double doors closing behind them. Wining dining and merry making ended soon after the climax of the evening as the guests began to dwindle away slowly. Our young waiter informed us our taxi was outside waiting to take us back home. What with the intoxicating cocktails and the jungle atmosphere my whole body was vibrating with excitement as we bade good night to the remaining guests.

Two months later my life had changed for the better as my association with Professor Fred Egan had now turned into a romantic interlude. Having my breakfast one morning a message was delivered to me by hand saying Mrs Phillips our old housekeeper was at death's door and would like to see me urgently before she departed this life. Responding immediately I went to a little village called Chandra to see her. On my arrival her neighbours ushered me into a darkened bedroom the only light being from a small bedside lamp. Seeing her lying there reminded me of my own poor mother who went to skin and bones before she died much the same plight as Mrs Phillips was in now. Entering the room she beckoned me to her bedside. Then what she told me in between fits of coughing and gasping for breathe frightened the living daylights out of me. She began telling me about my late parents.

"Your mother and father didn't die by natural causes. They were both helped on their way by Carla, and those black evil looking orchids she worships in the conservatory they are the work of the devil. After your poor mother's death your father would walk around the house as though he were in a trance. On many occasions when asking him if he required anything, only to be told in a polite manner, 'No thank you Mrs Phillips Carla will see to all my needs'.

After his marriage to Carla it was as though she controlled his every move, becoming more brazen with her general outlook on life. It was nothing to see her strutting about the house completely naked. One evening in particular your father had gone to bed early complaining of a bad migraine. Your step mother as usual was entertaining about twenty guests some women but mainly men. The whole bunch of them disappeared into the conservatory. Curiosity got the better of me and I peeked through the crack in the door. A strange music, the sound of which I had never heard before, was being played by one of her guests on a strange looking flute. Carla and all her guests were completely naked, dancing in front of those black orchids. The only light in the room being the moon shining through the glass roof. As they danced at certain intervals they would all stop, mumble in a strange dialect and get on their knees and kiss the floor in front of the flowers. Liquid from cups containing a thick white substance was being drunk. It might sound stranger than fiction, but it was like the flowers were controlling the dancers minds and bodies. Three young teenage girls lay naked on the floor in front of the orchids. . Neither one moved a muscle as they lay there, it was like they had been hypnotised or drugged. What happened next sent tremors of fear racing straight through my body. The whole gathering began chanting, the sound getting louder and louder to a fever pitch, and from my vantage point I saw the orchids root tentacles wrap themselves around one of the young girls legs dragging her towards the base of the plant. It was like a tug of war after that between the various orchids to see who could break off the biggest bit. It was horrible as those poor young girls were torn apart limb from limb and then digested into the main root of the plant. You know the whole gruesome spectacle frightened me half to death. I literally fled from that house. However going to the police with a strange story like that, who do you think they would believe Carla or me. They would think I had gone mental in my old age. What was even more terrifying more and more young people, men and women, were arriving from all over the world all being recruited to replace the ones being eaten. Jennifer the reason I;ve sent for you on my death bed, over the years I've seen you grow from a child into a beautiful woman. I can't go to my grave peacefully without warning you of the dangers, and your step mothers intentions towards you and your two daughters. Beware in an unguarded moment she will strike ending your lives, and giving her supreme power over everything. Your late fathers will made it clear the house should be divided equally between you and Carla but this arrangement doesn't suit her one little bit. She wants absolute power and nothing else will do. Plans have been made in their barbaric rituals to rid them of you for good. It's only a matter of time before you and your daughters will be lying face down naked in front of those evil plants, and also your husband Alec, he didn't run off with another women as the story was banded about. He loved you too much for that, he too was a victim. Through my cowardly actions a lot of young children have paid the supreme price. Now it's time to rid the world of that evil devil in disguise. When you confront your step mother Jennifer be on your guard at all times she has the looks and face of an angel but the mind of a monster.

At that last remark Mrs Phillips began coughing up blood, one of her friends dashed in to try and help, only to look at me and say, " it's too late she's gone Jennifer."

Thoughts of good times passed as I looked at Mrs Phillips for the last time with tear stained eyes. The blood in my veins boiling over with hatred. Thinking how my conniving step mother wanted to get rid of me that much, two can play at that game, biting my lip I murmured to myself.

Telephoning Fred I told him the whole gruesome story and my intentions. only to be told.

"You're not doing anything alone I'm coming with you," he quickly responded. Calling in at our local petrol station I purchased two plastic cans and filled them with petrol. Our plan was to get into the conservatory and pour petrol over Carla's precious black orchids and burn them. That would stop any of her wild plans for getting rid of my two daughters and me. Then we could slip quietly back home as though nothing had ever happened. Like all well laid plans there's normally a flaw in them. Fred and myself got into the conservatory without being detected and started the fires destroying the plants, flames from the fires engulfing them made them let out a high pitched sound. However on the way out we were confronted by my enraged stepmother and one of the guards. Then an almighty fight took place in the entrance hall. Teeth and talons were tearing the very clothes from off our bodies as we fought and wrestled with each other. Those cold hearted brown eyes of Carla's were spilling out hatred as she battled with me. It was a no win situation that I had got myself involved in. Flames from the conservatory fire had spread engulfing the rest of the house. For a woman in her middle sixties she fought like a wild tiger tearing flesh from my now naked body. Fighting tooth and nail it continued step by step up the stairs, then on the landing, all the time flames were licking around us as the old wooden staircase began to smoulder and burn. She was pure evil. You could see it in her eyes as she rested back, against the staircase bannister gulping in breath ready for the next assault on me. Leaning against the wall both of us were completely naked our bodies covered in blood and burn marks. As I watched her heaving chest going up and down. I realised there would be no such thing as compromise. It would be a fight to the death and I knew the outcome only too well. She was matching me punch for punch blow for blow.

The strength in my body was beginning to fail me, as we both stood facing each other on the stair landing gulping in precious air to resume the next onslaught. Bruises to my eyes had partly closed them, my mouth, nose, and face squirting out blood all were beginning to give me problems. Were Carla's naked body was like that of a young woman that's what alarmed me so much. She also had the stamina and strength to equal it. Breathing had become very heavy and difficult with the choking flames and toxic fumes. Looking at her through eyes now partly closed caused by blows to my face. I made one last desperate bid to end the conflict by charging at her with all my might sending us both crashing through the bannister onto the hall floor below. My logic was that if I'm about to die I'll make sure of one thing, I'm taking that evil monster with me. A telephone table in the hallway below, broke our fall, and also my stepmother's neck. Her naked body lay spread eagled over the floor underneath me. It was then with a loud bang the upper floor landing collapsed and came crashing down on top of me. That's all I remember until waking up in a hospital bed two days later with bruises and burns all over my body and a broken right leg.

At my trial, that made headline news, it's surprising the way a story of this magnitude is interpreted by the media but it did me no favours.

Witnessing the whole astonishing story being read out before a jury, only to be laughed out of court, the very thought was preposterous. Man eating orchids what ever next?. You will be telling us next, there were also little red men from Mars. Laughter around the court at those remarks sealed my fate. The public humiliation I had received had made me a laughing stock. A fireman who I owe my life to, made me blush as he read out his statement. Saying he had witnessed the fight between two naked women at the top of the stairs before both came crashing down. He gave an accurate account in his evidence of arriving at the scene to tackle the blaze. It was only by shear luck he had managed to drag my body clear of the inferno. Fred too had survived that night I'm glad to say. For my part in the whole charade, I was given eight years minimum to serve, and Fred for aiding and abetting me, three years.

During my stay in prison I decided it wouldn't get me down by attending the prison church services every Sunday, hoping one day my prayers would be answered and some one would come forward and explain to the authorities about the whole sordid episode. After the church service this Sunday I was given a message to report to the prison governors office at 9..00 o clock Monday morning. Standing there nervously waiting for him to arrive he waved a white piece of paper in his hands at me.

"New evidence has come to light in your particular case and this letter authorises me to release you immediately on parole until it's finds can be investigated thoroughly.

Six years to the day I had spent behind bars being caged like a wild animal and hearing those words sent tears flooding down my face.

Walking down the road free at last breathing in fresh air I never knew it could taste so good. I've paid the price for my crime and now its time to try and kick start my life once more. If someone had told me in my early years I would have served a term in prison in my lifetime for attempted murder I would never have believed them.

"Darling over here", a voice called out.

Oh I forgot to mention it, my future married name will be Mrs Frederick Egan we corresponded a lot between his visits to see me in prison.........

THE END

Grandmas Birthday Present

Flashing lights and the deafening sound of a wailing siren my body being bounced about from side to side. Traffic in the street blowing their horns loudly and pulling over to the side of the road, allowing the ambulance in which I was being transported, room to pass through. This was my dramatic entrance into the world. Some people are born into a world where everything is done for them, by the mere flick of one's hand the response is immediate. People like me, on the other hand, being born on the wrong side of the blanket have to scrimp and scrape all through life.

My first breath of life happened early one morning in an alleyway where my poor mother gave birth. Luckily for me, some passerby, a man out walking his dog, saw the predicament my mother was in and immediately telephoned for an ambulance. By a mere twist of fate and the exceptional skills of my rescuers, my life was saved but, alas, my mother died in the ambulance on the way to the hospital. On my birth certificate the space marked 'father' was followed by the word, "unknown". so I never knew him. All I know is that out there somewhere, a man is probably enjoying life with his family, never knowing of my existence. After spending six weeks in hospital wired up to a machine full of instruments, monitoring and recording my every move, I was finally released into my old grandma's charge. Right from the word go she took up the reigns and taught me how to survive in this world , and if I am allowed to blow my own trumpet, raised me into a fine good-looking intelligent young woman.

In those cherished years of my childhood living with my Grandma, memories of that era will stay in my mind until the day I die. My grandfather was killed in the war leaving my grandmother a widow, the only child of the marriage being my mother. We lived not in a big fancy house with servants at our beck and call, but in a street full of back to back terraced-type houses,where everyone knew everyone else's business. That is where I'm proud to say I grew up and that was my home.

Grandma's house was at the back of a block of four in what I can only describe as a small cobbled stone yard,having a wash house on the side all being shared with four more families. 'Privacy' a word some people couldn't even spell never mind understand. You could be having a soak in an old tin bath in front of the fire, the door would suddenly burst open leaving you red-faced and blushing, panicking, trying to cover up your private parts as one of our neighbours wanted a word with my Grandma. Situated at the top of the yard was the lavatory. This again had to be shared by four families. The 'posh' word for it now is toilet. Sometimes if you were lucky you could go straight in, otherwise it meant waiting in a small queue, discussing births and deaths with your neighbours,and hoping that the one in front of you hadn't been drinking too much. Sometimes the smell in there was overwhelming and you needed a gas mask !. I remember once having a spate of diarrhoea,where the pains in my stomach signalled an instant visit to the lavatory. Waiting in that endless and timeless queue as the pangs of pain caused me to criss-cross my legs, and thinking at the back of my mind; any moment now I'm going to fill my knickers.

The local comprehensive school that I attended, gave me the chance to show off my skills to my teachers and receiving top marks in every subject, and though I wasn't gifted with a silver spoon stuck in my mouth, my efforts and hard work paid off winning me a free scholarship to our local college.

To add another burden to our misery, the college rules stated I needed a uniform. This was easier said than done as when you are living on a fixed income you can't just wave your arms and money appears. It was usually a case of beg and borrow. My old

Grandma, being a pensioner, couldn't afford the expensive uniforms required, but was determined that I wouldn't lose out on this golden opportunity. Neighbours and friends got together some old clothes to provide me with a second hand uniform. Attending college,in my second hand; black blazer, skirt, jumpers, shirts, even my blue regulation knickers, but even in my poverty I felt ten feet tall. My old Grandma was a wizard at the sewing machine and had cut and fitted my clothes to perfection.

Every day going to college required me to find a small income to supplement my pocket money, so I applied at our local newsagents for a job as a paper girl. Mornings and evenings, I would change in and out of my college uniform and into my old clothes and deliver my newspapers. The bag might have been heavy, and the paper round long, but this gave me ample opportunity to read the comics, magazines and newspapers. Battling on through the long hot summer days of sunshine, and the dreary short cold days of winter, through rain,snow, blizzards and strong gales. Trudging around the streets every morning and evening with my heavy load. There was no such thing then as locked doors: it was a case of just walking through the doors and delivering hand-to-hand, occasionally stopping for a cup of tea or sampling someone's home made cake.

On a Sunday morning being rewarded for my efforts with a bigger round than normal also meant collecting in the money, and in doing so receiving some modest tips. These, with the help of my wages, provided me with enough money to help support myself. My grandma was well known in the area, and it was nothing in the growing season to return back home laden down with vegetables and fruit, which was all gratefully accepted.

Looking back over the years, my whole being fills up with emotion, tears pouring from my eyes thinking of that grey haired old lady and the things she taught me. Finishing my paper round especially in the cold wet winter nights, being tired, cold, hungry, and exhausted, my Grandma prided herself on her mouth watering-stews. Even thinking about them now makes me salivate. They satisfied me better than a four course meal, I quickly devoured them; it's surprising the way a cold snap in the weather makes your appetite swell.

She was old in years having her own little ways of saying things and her favourite past time was telling me fairy stories. These used to hold me spell-bound hanging on to her every word. Describing in vivid detail their features, body parts,and the clothes they wore. It was as though you were actually taking an active part in her stories. Some of her little characters wore yellow buttercups, and bluebells for caps. Some were dressed in pretty coloured leaves sewn together with golden or silver spider thread, and others wore tiny acorns for shoes ; I could go on all day!.

Parts of her stories used to send my imagination racing away into a fantasy world!. Certain times of the year, in a magical area in a garden, wood, or common a ring of toadstools would appear on the grass . These, she said, had bewitching properties and on such a night; when a full blue moon shone out of a star studded clear sky, fairies would come from miles around to dance around the ring of toadstools . Now at the stroke of midnight if a normal human being was lucky enough to find the ring of toadstools on this very special night, and stepped inside, turned around anti clockwise seven times, any wish they made would be granted.

Alas my Grandma died twenty eight days ago at the ripe old age of ninety four. Her parting has left me devastated. On my last visit to see her in the old folk's home, she reminded me of the days in my childhood and the stories she used to tell me. An old saying she used to brain-wash me with, was, 'even on the darkest of days if you look hard enough up into the heavens, a small shaft of light would shine through bringing you hope'. If only that were true and we could be like the fairies and live in never never land for ever and ever.

It 's my birthday and wedding anniversary in six days time ; Making it ten years since first I got wed, I have two small children by my marriage, Julie aged six, and Monica aged seven. They were both attending our local Infants school, where I have to trudge wearily twice a day to take them to and fro . This, as well as trying to hold down a job as a part time cashier at our local super market, which I'm glad to say in my present circumstances, isn't a thousand miles away, but only about 500 yards from the main school entrance.

Bad luck at this moment in time had reared it's ugly head. My husband had been confined to a hospital bed for the last twenty two months due to an injury received at his place of work. On my last visit to see him he gave me some alarming news. As well as the damage done to his back and legs they had found a growth at the base of his spine by his main spinal cord which could be cancerous. They say it never rains but pours, an old saying but quite true.

All my hopes of ever getting him back home and returning to a normal family life were shattered by this news. I felt like a ship at sea at the mercy of the rolling high waves in a storm, being smashed against the rocks. Leaving the hospital that night with my two children; It was like being paralysed, my whole body felt numb like someone in a trance ; there seemed no way forward and no hope for the future.

On these momentous occasions your mind drifts back to your childhood days for help and guidance. An old favourite saying of my Grandma's; 'A good shepherd always looks after his sheep'. Due to my husband's present circumstances he couldn't do a thing to help my two young daughters or me. All I know is that decisions and plans for the families future I had to make. It would be nice now and again, like in the old days, finding someone you could confide in, to ask for some friendly advice, but, alas, no one ever comes forward. Everyday racing about doing the same routine - it's starting to get me down. Getting up in the morning, going through the motions of preparing breakfast for myself and my darling unsuspecting daughters and then walking with them both to school. I was also doing my part time job to bring in enough money to buy food to eat. There's no such thing in this house as luxuries at this particular period in our lives. With regards to our clothes, it's a case of make do and mend; my Grandma taught me to cook, sew, and knit, all those years ago. This I am glad to say has worked wonders over the last few months. We have a small car but due to our financial difficulties at the moment we can no longer afford to run it, so it is standing idly on our drive.

My biggest headache and worry at this present moment in time is paying our bills. Every time I go shopping, items seem to keep going up by two or three pence. Household bills seem to be spiralling out of all control. Any day now I'm expecting the bailiffs to come around and repossess our home for failing to pay our mortgage. This, I know, would break my heart after having sunk all our savings into buying our home. Some mornings my eyes have been red raw from crying trying to find a solution to our problems. We have too many bills and little money to pay them. An old saying I've heard many times ; 'pay your debts and shame the devil', but how can you, when your meagre earnings don't even cover your food bill?. There is also the added expense of visiting my husband in hospital every night with our two children.

Today is my birthday. My two children sang me a birthday song at breakfast this morning which bought tears flooding into my eyes. Past birthdays have been times for celebration but not so this year. Then in the post a parcel for me, which read,

'To my dearest grandaughter Jessica, I've chosen this Fuchsia bush especially for your 30th birthday. Happy birthday, with all my love, Grandma'.

Tears came trickling out of my eyes as I looked at the Fuchsia bush. My Grandma must have ordered it for me before she died. I was determined to give it pride of place in my back garden. Taking our garden spade, and choosing a place , facing my kitchen window, the fuchsia bush was planted, so It could be admired by all.

Walking slowly back up the garden path to the kitchen I noticed a group of toadstools had appeared on our back lawn and they formed a perfect ring. These gave me an idea, what was my old grandmother's saying? .... "At the stroke of twelve midnight, step inside the magic ring, and by the light of a full blue moon, turn seven times anti clockwise and make a wish ". I made a solemn vow there and then it didn't matter how crazy it sounded - " this I will do tonight ".

Setting my alarm clock for eleven fifty five, and wearing only my night dress,I walked slowly down my garden path on that October night in what I can only describe as being the most magical part of my life. I've never seen the moon so big and blue in the sky its light illuminating the whole garden, moonbeams bombarding the lawn, stars twinkling in an inky blue sky.

Stepping carefully into the ring of toadstools, it didn't matter to me how crazy it sounded, desperate people do desperate things. The church clock began ringing out the chimes for midnight. Turning around seven times anti clockwise in that magic circle, crying and praying, I recited;

'Please, please, make my husband Tom well, so that he can leave hospital and we can be a family once again' !

Every morning during that next week I got into the habit of looking through the kitchen window at the Fuchsia bush. It was more like a morbid curiosity because I don't know what I expected to see;

Arriving in the post on the twenty eighth day of October, came a very official looking brown envelope. My heart was in my mouth, 'It's finally arrived', I thought to myself ' my eviction notice for failing to keep up the payments on our mortgage'. My whole body trembled so much I just couldn't face opening it. Even when taking my two children to school,whether or not my present circumstances had dulled my senses I shall never know, I kept getting the strange impression that everyone was trying to avoid me. Seeing a friendly face, and then in the blinking of an eye they were gone. That anonymous brown envelope arriving in the mornings post was like a nightmare coming true. I was already imagining the bailiffs turning my two children and myself out onto the streets with nowhere to go, our precious belongings being piled up out side for all to see.

Nerves all tattered and in shreds, returning home that night and grabbing the brown envelope I tore it open and read its contents. It was from a solicitor in our towns high street .... Scripps, Scripps, & Scripps. All it read was.......

An appointment has been made for you to attend this office

on Friday third of November 2007 at 4..30pm would you please attend ?.

My biggest nightmare was about to come true. Focusing my eyes on its contents; it didn't matter how I tried, my hands would not stop shaking. In bed that night my nerves were all on edge. Sleeping was impossible, tossing and turning; I was making myself sick with worry. Early next morning my husband was due to have an operation and so I couldn't burden him with any more worries. This was my problem and I had to solve it.

Friday arrived all too soon and I carried out my daily routine of household chores. After collecting my children from school and still in a daze, we managed to find our way to the solicitor's office and sat patiently in the reception area. It took all of my strength to hold back the tears to stop me crying I was so upset. We were all ushered into a big office full of files piled on top of one another, it was like something from a Dickens novel. At once taking a defensive stance, handing the solicitor my mortgage payment book, I began sobbing as I tried to get the words out explaining to the solicitor my present predicament . Indicating with his hand he said in a gentle manner,

'Hush.... hush'.

" Your name is Jessica Henderson, Grandaughter of the late Mrs Martha Henderson Is this true.?"

Answering him, nervously I could hardy get the words out,

" Yes sir that is correct".

Mr Scripps was an old man of slim build with a wisp of grey hair trying to cover a bald crown, his glasses hung precariously on the end of his nose.

Fiddling with some papers and putting them in their correct order once again and pointing with his fingers he addressed me, "Give me that mortgage book and I will deal with it for you". As he spoke on the telephone, I was trembling so much I only caught snatches of the conversation,

"There", he said speaking with a smile, " that's one problem solved at least", putting the telephone back on the receiver.

"A distant relative of your late grandma has left her a legacy, to be precise a large sum of money from the sale of a property she owned".

Looking at him I questioned his last remark ."What has that got to do with me?".

"We have been tracing back through official records and the last remaining live member of your grandma's family is you. I have mediated on your behalf and settled your mortgage account leaving a balance on the legacy, that will be paid to you in full immediately the sum is £20,000 pounds".

Handing me the cheque had rendered me speechless. Looking at this life saver he had just handed me, was I still in the land of the fairies? Things like this don't happen in real life, especially to people like me.

Visiting my husband in hospital that evening with my two children I was bursting at the seams waiting to tell him my good news, Tom was so excited as I approached him he sat up at a slight angle in bed. His facial expression stretched from ear to ear with a big beaming smile. He couldn't even wait for me to kiss him as he blurted out his good news.

"This morning the operation carried out by the doctors was removing a tumour from my spine. It isn't cancerous - it was a large abscess! It has taken the pressure off my spinal cord and I can now move my toes - look!" He was so excited he pulled the bedclothes back and showed me. Trying to enter into the conversation with my good news was almost impossible. It felt as though someone had removed a large weight off my shoulders.

" In two days time I'm starting a course of treatment which will eventually get me back on my feet, Jessica. This is the best news we've had in ages! This means I will be coming back home!"

Hearing my husband's tremendous news, a flood of tears came streaming down my face. This put the inheritance money out of my mind. My good news would wait until another day.

On that November night, as I walked down my garden path at midnight, it was cold, dark, damp the church clock had just struck twelve. It's echoes vibrating the air around me in the darkness.   Looking at the Fuchsia bush my Grandma had bought me and with the tears pouring from my eyes.

"...... Thank you........ Thank you....... Thank you".

I kept repeating to myself over and over again

THE END

THE AMOROUS CAVALIER

Ghost is a word that conjures up in my mind the figure of a man or woman from bye-gone day's, gliding effortlessly like a mist or shadow in dimly lit area's like corridors, or rooms, in medieval ruins. They say a cold spot in a certain part of the building signifies a ghostly presence, or things that go bump in the night, or items of furniture being rearranged. Speaking for myself I have never encountered such goings on I'm glad to say.

Two months ago my life was torn apart, at the death of my husband Roy leaving me devastated, who died from a massive heart attack at the age of forty- one. He had been working harder than normal to complete some orders for his customers, and after finishing work one night he decided to take a bath before his evening meal. Little did I know as I watched him walk up the stairs that it would be the last time I would see him alive. We made many plans in our first months of marriage but no one ever plans for these unforeseen circumstances. Hermione our only child of the marriage, alas was born with Downs Syndrome. This made my life even more complicated, looking after her is a full time job with her attendance at special schools and training.

Someone once told me that everyone has their own special guardian angel watching over them. If only that were true. In my present circumstances what I needed desperately was a live-in job to support my widows pension and stop my hard earned savings from slowly dwindling away. Paying my mortgage now my husband had gone was out of the question. My husband's catering business supplied restaurants and hotels with their essential supplies but at his death that too had now ceased to exist, leaving me a lonely widow at thirty seven with a Downs Syndrome daughter,who I love and endeavour to support. One of my late husband's many customers, upon hearing of my present predicament, offered me a job in one of their many hotels to work on the managerial staff team, as a liaison officer and trouble shooter resolving the guests problems. Knowing my love of history, had also asked me if I would like to act as an official guide and give conducted tours in their new five hundred bed-roomed complex. It was like a fairy tale coming true. The hotel was an old mansion house converted into bedrooms, sitting rooms, dining rooms, pool and sports and leisure facilities. There was a large pavilion built on the side to host an array of different cabarets and shows nightly. To top it all, my living accommodation; was a two bed roomed flat built away from the guests bedrooms at the far end of the hotel, this was all accessible by a long corridor, now what more could a person hope for !.

With my natural wit and humour I soon got into the swing of my new job, putting the newly arrived guests at ease by pointing out things of importance and places of interest to visit during their stay. Being the official guide and having a natural flair to be in the spotlight, with my own special brand of humour, I could put the guests' minds at ease and roll away the clouds of darkness and despair. By telling them spine tingling yarns about our new acquisition and some slightly risque' jokes thrown in for good measure I had them rolling about with laughter.

Bookings for reservations were coming in fast and furious from far and wide. Some of our guests after enjoying a pleasant week in our hotel were re-booking, twice, three, and even four times a year. That's how popular we had become in such a small space of time!

Meeting them all personally every day and sorting out their teething problems was all part of a days work for me.

Speaking for myself, I pride myself for having taken care of my figure and having remained quite trim. My hazel eyes, and short brown hair with a fringe at the front all enhanced my beauty. My full name is, Elizabeth Allison Dolittle. The guests had nicknamed me Liza which quite amused me, and though I had friends none had shown me the familiarity as the guests did I felt quite at home.

Workmen were carrying out repairs in our underground basement one day and sent me a very excited message that called for my presence immediately. Knocking down some old brickwork in our basement to make way for some new storage shelves, had revealed two smaller rooms off the main cellar. One was full of old dogeared books, and paintings. The other had a small bricked up alcove like a dungeon used to detain prisoners. Articles of clothing, including some old buttons and buckles were found. Realising the importance of our find had caused a great deal of excitement among my superiors. Very soon four smartly dressed men arrived from our head office to inspect our newly found antiquities. Seeing the wonderful collection of paintings and books they decided on a big publicity drive by getting them all cleaned and restored to their former glory. Then hanging the paintings, five in all, at the top of a big open stairway leading up to some of the more expensive bridal suites in the hotel. Pride of place was given to one painting in particular. The one, a full length painting of a Cavalier measuring eight foot by six.

A new task was assigned to me, "Liza we have been studying your CV and noticed, you have a diploma in history. We would like you to find out as much as possible about our new mysterious paintings. Scout around the local villages and churches leave no stone unturned and get some help if you need it. Let's see if we can find out the owners of these mysterious paintings and turn the whole business into a spectacular publicity stunt for the hotel. On the original deeds and papers the old Mansion house purchased by us belonged to the Darcy family making the property three to four hundred years old ! It would be nice if the past were investigated to find out what actually happened here! "See what you can do". I was glad to undertake this new venture anything to fill in some of my spare time, as a lot of it was spent mourning Roy.

Researching the paintings history, plus my extra chores kept me very busy indeed, so it came as a bit of a shock, four days later after the discovery, when one of the builders came to me very concerned, complaining that when they finished work for the day, all their tools were locked in a room in the basement. However on their return the following morning the tools were strewn all over the floor. I hadn't got an answer for this particular incident, but I would certainly mention it to the hotel security guards.

Standing on the bottom of the beautiful marble staircase and admiring our new requisitions of the five restored paintings, the picture that really caught my eye and sent my imagination going haywire, was the one of the dashing, handsome and enigmatic Cavalier. Three were portraits of what could have been members of his family, his father, mother, and sister. A forth showed the old mansion house in its hay day hundreds of years ago.

Looking up at the paintings and murmuring to myself I asked; " Who are you and what are you doing here?", I was determined to get to the bottom of this mystery and find the answers to my many questions.

There was also found in the cellar some old books and documents, a bit worse for wear, but by using some modern technology I was able to start to piece the jigsaw puzzle together. Writing down in detail with the help of sketches, and logging all my finds, checking parish records and visiting burial sites, around the old house and asking the local people if they could help me in any way.

At the end of six months my hard labour had paid off and I was able to write a complete report on my findings. At a special board meeting convened by the directors. I was able to explain the history of the old mansion house leading up to the present day.

My search for the truth had led me on a three hundred year old love story about the handsome young Cavalier in the huge painting hanging at the top of the marble stair-case. It turned out to be Sir Rupert De-la-Wynter eldest son of Sir Robert and Isabel De-la-Wynter. Rupert was an officer in the King's cavalry being mentioned many times in dispatches for acts of heroism during the civil war between the Cavaliers and the Round heads. He was also a soldier of fortune gathering great wealth for his family during his many adventures and escapades. Records suggested he was in love with a Christina Darcy, and planned to marry her at the end of the civil war. However the war took a turn for the worse with the king's army being defeated by the Round heads. There had always been bitter rivalry and feuding between the two families. The Darcy family had supported the Roundhead cause and at the end of the conflict had demanded their neighbours house and lands by right of conquest. Sir Rupert, a tall, attractive and gallant young man, was forever getting himself into trouble with jealous husbands over their wives throwing themselves at his feet. His weakness for beautiful women was to be his downfall, one such episode ended up in a duel to the death with his neighbour, Sir Walter Darcy after he had been found in bed with Christina. This resulted in Sir Walter being killed outright and members of his family, in a revenge attack, thrust their rapiers into Sir Rupert. Two more members of the Darcy family were also wounded in this frenzied attack. Sir Rupert managed to drag himself, blood stained and barely alive back home where he collapsed on the doorstep,dying in his fathers arms. Fearing further attacks from the Darcy family, his body was hidden and entombed in a small alcove in the cellar. Everything of any value was also hidden in an underground room adjacent to the cellar of the Mansion house.

Members of the Darcy family had now taken the opportunity to attack and seize their neighbours house and lands. By failing to disclosed the whereabouts of Sir Ruperts body the whole De-la-Wynter family and their servants were systematically tortured and murdered in retaliation for the death and injuries inflicted on their family. Consequently all lands belonging to the De-la-Wynters were now forfeited and were seized by their rival family. Rupert's sweetheart, Christina Darcy when told of the terrible murders and of what had happened reported the crime to

Cromwell's soldiers who metered out their own punishment on the perpetrators of this foul act. Christina heartbroken over the death of her lover was later found hanging from a tree for her part in the whole shady affair. Over the years the old house has had many owners, the latest being the last living member of the Darcy family.

A dossier has been compiled by myself explaining in detail the terrible events in this sordid story. So our mystery paintings at the top of the staircase as suspected was Sir Rupert De-la-Wynter and the other four, his Mother, Father, Sister and the old Mansion house.

Hearing this story bought a rapturous applause from the gathering upon which Liza was promoted to Assistant Manager and with a salary increase. News of the story generated a lot of publicity in the media for the hotel. The open marble staircase was renamed the Cavalier's Staircase.

Full to capacity the hotel was bursting at the seams, with advanced bookings being made well into the future. Everyone visiting the hotel wanted to walk up the famous Cavalier's staircase and have their photograph taken by Sir Rupert's painting.

One day, as Liza was relaxing, having a well earned drink in the hotel cafeteria, she accidentally overheard a conversation at the table opposite between six middle aged ladies. One lady an attractive blonde was explaining to her friends a strange experience that happened in her room the previous night, after leaving the ballroom. Pointing to a slim brunette sitting at her side, she related,

" My friend Paula and I share a twin bedded room, whatever she was drinking last night I certainly want some". This comment bought a roar of laughter from her friends.

"I woke up and found the room itself was as light as day, being illuminated by a beautiful silvery full moon. Looking over to her bed, Paula's stark naked body lay on top of the sheets. Her breathing was heavy and her chest and body going up and down as if someone was making love to her ! Rubbing my eyes I thought they were playing tricks on me. Her sweat covered body was twisting and contorting in front of me on the bed, it didn't seem possible, we were the only two in the room. Slowly I pulled the sheets back over her naked body, awakening her could have been fatal !".

In the following months I heard similar stories told by different guests in different parts of the hotel. One told me, in the strictest confidence about an incident happening in the bathroom, a women in her middle thirties drying herself off after a shower glancing in the mirror to admire her figure felt a sixth sense told her she wasn't alone, " But the bathroom was empty, I just can't explain it",

She said to me, " I could feel someone's eyes monitoring my every move".

What had started off as someone's erotic sexual fantasy had now become a regular occurrence. We feared repercussions of our mysterious phenomenon, and bookings being cancelled , it had the adverse effect however, more, and more, people were arriving on hearing stories circulated about the romantic exploits of our mysterious ghost.

Hermione was now eighteen and I was given permission by my superiors to hold a special birthday party for her with some of my friends and the guests at the hotel. Everyone was very generous with the presents she received. There was a look of sheer delight on her face as she opened every one. She loves to dance and the hotel band had no trouble in playing her kind of music and being full of bounce she soon wore me out. Dancing in the middle of the floor on her own, one of my friends tapped me on the shoulder and remarked,

" Who is Hermione talking to?", even I looked puzzled. Her hands were held up high as if she was dancing with someone taller than herself. Her little mouth was talking ten to the dozen as she waltzed around the floor. Seeing her enjoying herself so much, other couples decided to join her on the dance floor and enjoy the music.

Putting her to bed that night I casually asked,

" who were you talking to and dancing with on the ballroom dance floor?". Her reply knocked me flat and rendered me speechless .

"That was Rupert Mom. He said I was the prettiest and best dressed lady in the ballroom and could he have the honour of dancing with me and being my escort".

This last comment from my daughter sent my whole body into shock, trembling with fear. I questioned her more fully on the subject. " Rupert who? what does he look like?"

Putting on her dressing gown and taking me by the hand,

" I'll show you", Leading me down the corridors, Hermione stopped at the bottom of the Cavalier's staircase, "that's him, look Mom" , pointing at the painting of Sir Rupert De -la- Wynter. Shocked, it took me all my strength to control my horror, gazing at the painting the gleam in his eye looked as though he were smiling deviously straight back at me. That night as I lay in my bed, his facial expression would not leave my mind, try as I may, sleep would not come. Had all my hard work been too much for me?, or was this a mere trick of my eyes?. Tossing and turning going over and over in my mind all night, Hermione's weird experiences. Ghosts don't exist in real life, it's someone's bizarre imagination that makes them appear, I kept telling myself over and over again. What makes things worse, why is it she can see him and nobody else can? It doesn't make any sense at all.

A week later I was asked to organise a special banquet and reception for one of the older member's of our staff on his retirement. Leaving Hermione in the loving care of one of my friends for the evening, on my return I thanked my friend very much for the favour and a comment she made gave me goose bumps all over.

"She has been playing on her computer all night, I've been keeping a watchful eye on her, I swear the way she's been acting, she wasn't alone".

Hermione was playing on her computer as I looked through the crack in the door. An empty chair placed right next to her was her only companion she was too pre-occupied with talking to someone else to notice I had returned. Phrases like "Rupert you're cheating!" then fits of laughter from her. Whoever she was talking to was certainly amusing her. Inching my way into the room and behind Hermoine's chair. What I saw next nearly froze the blood in my veins. The keys on the computer were working themselves making the images on the screen come to life. "Who is in this room beside you young lady!" I demanded.

Answering me " it's Rupert Mom can't you see him sitting on that chair next to me. Slowly sliding my hand in the direction of the chair it felt as though it had just been put into a fridge.

"Rupert doesn't mean you any harm Mom, he likes playing games with me on my computer " came Hermonie's innocent reply.

Looking at the joy in that little girl's face, I didn't want to spoil it, I've never known her so happy; since her father died. An assistant manager's job is a very demanding one, having very little time to play games and amuse her. Someone from a bye-gone age had now come on the scene and taken my place, who only the little girl can see, and he too was lost in his own time warp. Her happy little face decided me there and then that if you can't beat them join them. "Come on young lady its well past your bedtime, say good night to your friend. A movement in the air signalled to me our ghostly friend had departed.

I've read stories in books and magazines of ghosts, haunting old houses and frightening people half to death, but never in a million years ever thought of encountering one. What was even stranger was this mysterious Cavalier had befriended my daughter. It's an impossible situation to be in, but without causing any more unhappiness and grief I would just have to accept the inevitable. Seeing the pleasure they both got out of the computer games I took the liberty of ordering some more. No more reports were filtering back to me of Ruperts amorous advances, I'm glad to say, and everything was starting to get back to normal or at least as close to normal as you can get with a friendly computer-literate ghost in your life!

123

Hermione had been complaining about pains in her stomach and chest so I made an appointment for her to see our local GP. He immediately after his examination whisked her off to the nearest hospital, and much later, after a large number of tests had been carried out. The doctor informed me she had a fast growing cancerous tumour. It would only be a matter of weeks before it would take over and take my little girl from me. There was nothing they could do about it. Devastated at the news I had just received, my head was in a spin. At once I applied for a leave of absence to stay at the hospital with my precious daughter. Every second of each passing day felt like a count down to the inevitable. On that final morning looking at her cold still young body through my tear stained eyes, sharp pains went shooting through my whole body making my head spin around and around rendering me unconscious.

Next thing I remember was looking up at a young doctor leaning over me. He gave me more alarming news, my daughters condition had triggered a near fatal heart attack in me, but to add to the agony, tests had also been carried out while I had been unconscious for the last two days, revealing and growing at an incredible rate inside my body were two fast growing cancerous cells. After a week of being prodded night and day and having countless needles thrust into me I was finally released to bury my darling daughter.

Inside the church on the day of the funeral were scores of young children from Hermione's school all with tear filled eyes paying their last respects. Our local priest conducting the service gave a beautiful sermon accounting for some important events in Hermione's life. They say the sun only shines on the righteous, this is quite true I have never seen so many people at a funeral the church was full to overflowing, there were even people listening to the service outside.

Returning back to my flat after weeks of absence, it felt cold and damp inside even on this warm summer's day. Events in my life over the last few weeks had shattered all my plans for the future into a thousand fragments. Sitting on the corner of my bed tears pouring down my face, a cold draught reminded me I wasn't alone in the room. Speaking into the silence of that empty room,

"Rupert, Hermione, won't be coming back. She died in hospital a few weeks ago and she was buried this morning. Over the past months you have brought a great deal of laughter and happiness into her world of silence. I can never thank you enough for that. My life too is also hanging on a fine wire I'm dying, from an incurable disease, and I too will depart from this world in a couple of months. Before my final demise I want you to know that we have found the remains of a mass grave in the woods, which we believe could be your family and servants. In the alcove in which you were imprisoned enough materials ,dust , debris and particles of clothing have been found to bury your last remains in your parents grave so that you can all be reunited once again, otherwise you will be all alone and trapped in the 21st century. I've arranged for our local hotel chaplain to conduct your burial service and give you a blessing. This last gesture from me is to reward you for making a little girls life complete with your gentlemanly charms and grace. I too, like you will also be reunited in the same grave as my husband and daughter, in a matter of weeks. The name of Elizabeth Allison Doolittle will soon be forgotten but your name and your amorous exploits will live on until the end of time itself. The stories handed down from mother to daughter will never die........ So good bye and goodluck, Sir Rupert De-la-Wynter".

The End

The Devil Cat

It's nice just once in a while to let your mind drift back in time to those happy days of our childhood, when we were young. Recently I took my two young grandchildren to our local zoo which bought childhood memories from the past flooding back. My Mother and Father made it an annual event to take me to the Zoo at least once a year, to watch the antics of the different animals as they paraded around their compounds. There my father, with his vast superior knowledge of the world, would explain in fine detail the habitats and countries the various animals came from. By using his hands he had his own special way of expressing himself. This sent a thrill of excitement right through my body when I was young, clinging on to his every word .

Looking at the expressions of delight on my two grandchildren's faces was a pleasure as we watched the Monkeys and Chimpanzees swinging through the air on the branches of trees. Then, explaining in detail to them where the various animals came from just like my father did for me when I was young.

"Grandma what kind of animals are those the one's with the black and orange strips"?, my excited little grandson said jerking my skirt.

Smiling down at him I said, "Those are Tigers and they are only found in Asia, living in the hills and jungles". One of the Tigers, a female, had two cubs whom she was playing with and guarding against any intrusion. It reminded me a little of my role in life looking after my two grandchildren while their mother was out at work all day. Seeing those big cats in that enclosure jogged part of my memory about an incident that happened on an island in the pacific in the war years.

Writing short stories and sketching is a part time hobby of mine. Finding the characters for my stories from real life rather than inventing them, and getting them involved in a do or die situation revolving around a plot . A story told to me recently about the events on a remote pacific island in world war two sent the blood rushing around my body at an alarming rate. When you write fictional stories you have to imagine your characters and their environment in your mind . However a real life drama told to you by a person who actually lived through the horrifying saga leaves you breathless.

Holiday photographs in those glossy travel brochures and magazines have always had a magnetic fascination for me, especially one in particular: The beautiful island of Ilonowa in the South Pacific. Pictures of this island of enchantment have held me spell-bound for years. Always hoping that one day good fortune would shine on my husband and I, and we could raise enough funds to go and spend a holiday there. There's an old saying from the past, if you wish for a something long enough it invariably comes true. Someone at last has answered my wish. Upon my retirement after spending forty years slaving over a type-writer and doing my firms wages, my employers rewarded me for my loyal service, with two tickets for a months vacation on the island of Ilonowa. You often dream about these moments, but never in a million years expect them to come true. Looking at those tickets and then at my employers sent tears flooding down my cheeks. It was like a fairy tale coming true. Shaking them strongly by the hand and thanking them very much for their kind hospitality.

Dreams are wonderful for capturing that warm glowing feeling of being in never- never land, until you have to wake up. You can spend a lifetime planning a visit to a favourite spot on the map and once there it is all over in a flash leaving you only with it's treasured memories. In my particular circumstance this was quite true. My dream Island in the pacific was certainly worth the wait. Like all good things you wait a life time for, in the twinkling of an eye it's all over. This is a month in my life I shall treasure until the day I die, but alas, it was all ending this very weekend. As my husband and I attended a memorial service in a lovely stone built church in the beautiful harbour town of Ilonowa in the South pacific, tomorrow would be our last day to enjoy the fruits of this tropical island paradise, before the dream bubble bursts and we are whisked off, by boat to the mainland, and then a flight back home to reality.

During our stay on this beautiful pacific island paradise words, just can't describe its panoramic beauty. Every minute of every day, whether on sight seeing excursions or visiting historical places of interest, both of us enjoyed its pleasures to the full. It didn't matter in what location we were, or who's company we were in. Two names would inevitably slip into the conversation, 'Suki , and, The Devil Cat'. Whenever these names were mentioned our tour guides would stick out their chests with pride . This reaction caught my imagination and goes far beyond the boundaries of reality making me more determined than ever to find out more about this devil cat. Even after all this time just thinking about it brings tears to my eyes.

On our last day of our magical holiday my curiosity got the better of me and I asked the hotel manager about the names, Suki, and The Devil Cat, and what they meant. He explained to me, in broken English, that he had only been manager there but a short time. An Indian lady named Naomi who lived in a large white painted house only a mile from the hotel on the coast road could probably give me the answers to all my questions.

Following the hotel managers instructions to the letter. My husband and I arrived outside a large white painted house. Palm tree plants decorated the driveway leading up to the front door. An attractive, slim, elderly Indian lady answered our knock on the door. Her long flowing grey hair glistening in the morning sun as it hung down over her shoulders. She was wearing a long plain white summer dress with some beads sown into the neck line which rebounded the suns rays.

"Excuse me", I said very politely," I'm looking for a lady named Naomi?".

" Look no further you have found her, that is I", she answered with a lovely smile.

I introduced myself and my husband, and explained the nature of my visit. She made a gesture with her hand and bade me enter. Her voice was soft and tender and she spoke in a perfect polished English accent.

" My Husband Bill and I have been staying on your beautiful Island for nearly a month and today is our last day before returning home. During our many sight seeing tours and parties two names kept creeping frequently: into the many conversations. " Can you please explain to me why the name, 'Suki ', and The 'Devil cat ' bear so much importance and significance to the people of this Island?". I asked her in rather a shy manner.

Smiling back at me, she asked me if we would like to join her for some refreshments in her garden then she would tell me the story. We accepted her kind offer and sat down on chairs, on a large white patio. Everywhere looked like a travel brochure, with tropical flowers showing off their dazzling array of colours. Birds and monkeys were in the palm trees. Naomi brought Bill and myself a cool refreshing orange drink in two large slim glass and then sat down facing us.

"Suki, and The devil cat, you say?, they are both one of the same. To the people of this island that name will live on until the end of time itself, she then began telling me her remarkable story..........

After receiving a much sort after college degree in India in 1938, I was now the proud owner of a diploma in foreign languages, my ambition was to be an interpreter and travel and see as much of the world as possible in my lifetime. To my utter surprise, a job was advertised in our local newspaper, for an interpreter to act as a liaison officer and work in a province in Northern India for a British engineering company.

After applying for the position and sending off my qualifications never thinking in a million years I would get the post, to my surprise, a letter came in the post a few days later offering me the job, which I at once accepted. My new employer was a civil engineer working on a huge building project in Northern India. I had been hired as an interpreter and liaison officer to communicate with the work force and explain in detail what was required of them and help sort out any teething problems, as they were of many creeds and nationalities.

Mr John Williams my new employer, was a very tall smart looking man. He was there with his wife Susan, and their two girls, Janet aged twelve and the youngest, Rebecca aged eight, who I'm sorry to say was badly deformed, and had to rely on a crutch to enable her to walk. She had been born with a twisted right leg, and in her few short years of life had also developed problems in her left shoulder which became badly arched. With all her deformities, she was a very pleasant and likable child and we got on like a house on fire spending many, many, happy hours together playing games reading books, and reciting poetry .

One of the workers on the site presented Rebecca with a very tiny Tiger cub. It had been found abandoned by it's mother wandering in the bush. The poor little thing was so thin and scrawny we all doubted if it would last the night, but we hadn't reckoned on the love and grim determination shown by her new found mistress as she cuddled and nursed the little cub back to health. In the months ahead as the young cub grew they were inseparable. Rebecca and her new found friend both enjoying the delights of each other's company.

It came like a bolt out of the blue , when one morning Mr Williams called me into the site office and told me he had been offered a new position on the Island of llonowa in the South Pacific and asked me if I would like carry on my job as liaison officer and go with him and his family and live there. I couldn't get the words out quick enough, "Yes please!". came my answer in a flash. All my dreams of seeing the world were coming true: now was my big chance. During my present employment every week my pay slip had money deducted for my parents back home. When they heard my good news, they were over the moon.

Ilonowa was a large tropical island in the pacific, with it's many plantations dotted everywhere growing every thing from tea to pineapples. It's large natural harbour was surrounded on two sides by a very quaint stone-built coastal town. Mr William's firm had been hired to build a new hotel in the coastal town and to improve, widen and deepen the entrance into the harbour, so opening up the island to bigger ships and tourism. This house I'm living in had been specially built for him and his family. By now I was treated as one of the family occupying the guest room . When we first arrived here the people who lived on the island were a divided lot. Some had Christian beliefs, others believed in the old rituals of black magic and voodoo. We were treated like intruders but as the months progressed they began to accept us for what we were.

Rebecca wouldn't leave her little cub behind so, she too was brought to the island . Over the next few years we witnessed a scrawny little cub turn into a beautiful female tiger. Rebecca and Janet would take, Suki, that is what the girls had named her, out each day on a lead and walk with her down the many winding pathways to the sandy beaches. Big as ,Suki, was, it was like having a huge guard dog on a lead. She made no attempt to stray from Rebbeca's side as she walked patiently down the paths to the sandy beaches below. Anyone approaching from the opposite direction gave them a wide birth. The mere sight of those huge teeth and claws was enough to send a shiver down the spine of even the bravest amongst them. The native people of the island had never seen a Tiger before so due to her size and colour in their own superstitious beliefs they nicknamed her, 'the devils cat' . Tigers are not afraid of water so the well developed big cub and the two girls, once on the beach would gambol and frolic about in the surf for hours on end. Sometimes on my days off I would accompany them down to the beach making sure I stayed out of Suki's way, as a full grown Tiger shaking the water out of fur sends the sea water cascading in all directions actually soaking the person nearest to her. It was also an ideal opportunity for me to make some sketches of the three of them playing in the sea together. Scenes like that are rarely forgotten .

A large compound had been specially erected on the side of the house to keep Suki in as she was now a full grown female tiger standing about four feet to the top of her back, and so domesticated it was nothing to see her walking around the house. Rebbeca had chosen the name Suki for her, I've watched, with tears rolling down my cheeks with laughter, as the two of them rolled about on the floor together. Rebbeca would roll the big cat over and over and then tickle her tummy, Suki was like a big, soft, cuddly toy.

There was only one problem with Suki: she was deaf and dumb from birth, and to catch her attention you had to try and catch her eye. Then you had to brace yourself as she came bounding over. She loved her ears and head stroked, you could do it all day and she wouldn't mind. Her coat of orange with black stripes was beautifully marked.

In 1939, the war began in Europe. We seemed comparatively safe on our desert island paradise but not for long . Every day the news got worse and worse as the enemy gobbled up and over-ran each country in turn. It saddened our hearts when Britain was left, fighting for her very existence alone, to fight the war.

Even more alarming news reached us in the December of 1941: The Japanese had bombed the American naval base at Pearl Harbour and were sweeping through the Pacific like a tidal wave. We knew in our hearts the way they were advancing it wouldn't be long before they came knocking on our door. A militia was formed from the islands inhabitants to try and defend our island home and fend off our invaders.

One morning in the late summer of 1942, the truth became a reality as Japanese dive bombers began bombing the harbour defences and naval gun fire began devastating the harbour town. Then they came storming ashore from three separate landing points, killing and shooting everything in sight. A lot of innocent people men women and children, were killed in those first few days of hostilities, as we tried in vain to defend our home against the invader.

Among the many casualties of war, were, Mr and Mrs Williams and their two children. By a strange twist of fate, the bombs that had hit the back part of the house killing the family had also wrecked the tiger's compound setting her free to roam at will. Even now thinking about it my hands were red raw as I feverishly pulled and tugged at woodwork and masonry to find their bodies.

If I live for a hundred years I shall never forget the day we buried all the bodies of our friends and loved one's in our local cemetery. There was certainly quite a few. Our new masters stood by shouting and jeering at us.

A very strange thing then happened.... the monkeys and birds, normally chattering away, were suddenly silent; EVERYTHING....went deathly quiet. A Japanese soldier leaning against a tree had been sent to guard us He was there one minute and gone the next. I couldn't believe my own eyes rubbing them to try and clear my vision. A search was made of the whole area, but nothing was ever found. He had just vanished.

After that particular incident our new masters watched us like hawks, making us work long hours without a break. They were brutal and overwhelming task masters: one word out of turn - it didn't matter how insignificant - meant a beating, or death. They kept us prisoners in an old school house. The women on the inside and the men outside.That too had taken a direct hit in the bitter conflict and so when it rained, the rain came cascading down from the holes in the roof .

One night in the moonlight looking through an open window, I could see the crosses in the church yard on all the newly dug graves. There was a lonely figure silhouetted against the moon standing vigil over the graves of Mr Williams and his family: it was Suki. She was so confused, she hadn't got a clue what was going on.

These unforeseen circumstances had turned a lovable domesticated big cat into a deadly silent killer and man eater. In the months ahead the Japanese would find out to their peril what they had unleashed on this sleepy South Pacific island.

133

The second incident I recall to mind was when six Japanese soldiers where bathing in that lovely clear blue sea. It must have felt like heaven on earth after finishing their tour of duty for the day, splashing about in the cool water without a care in the world. As they walked up the beach after frolicking about in the surf, they never knew what hit them as the big cat suddenly sprung from hiding, her teeth and claws ripping their bodies to shreds. No one survived the attack.... one body was dragged into the bush and never seen again.

Our oppressors were furious at this outrage and tried to find an explanation for these sudden deaths. They rounded us all up in the town square, beating women and children alike. No one was spared. We told them it was a Tiger. They only laughed and scoffed at our pathetic replies: and beat us more and more. One of the male prisoners died that night from the awful beatings.

"There are no Tigers on these Islands,! " You think we are fools?," came a Japanese officer's furious reply.

Patrols were sent into the jungle to try and root out the perpetrator only to find on their return to camp more of their comrades were missing. On this island of Ilonowa was like a Tiger's paradise. Mountains, and valleys densely wooded with thick undergrowth. Open spaces had been hacked out of the jungle for its many plantations. A shore line with overgrown green foliage stretched for miles.

Two weeks later we were all herded together like sheep in the main square of the town. Japanese soldiers had formed a guard of honour on the two sides. While their superior officer stood on a platform in front and addressed us. After our lecture by him on the, do's and don'ts, he returned to his quarters and was never seen again. It was becoming a nightly occurrence to hear a guard suddenly scream out with fright, followed by rifle and machine gun fire as Suki prowled around looking for easy prey. Standing guarding strategic positions the soldiers were easy targets so her killing spree went on . Moving through the under growth and taking advantage of the dark shadows she was like a phantom hardly moving a blade of grass, blending perfectly into her nightly surroundings. Being a mute, she made no sound at all, so her reign of terror continued unchecked.. People of the island being reaped in superstition and not knowing what she was had given her the name 'The devils cat'. This was the name the Japanese had now decided to call her. The strange irony of it all?. Suki was as free as a bird to roam where she pleased. She had no boundaries,and while the rest of us were held prisoners we were little more than slaves doing our masters bidding. We were being marched out every morning onto a make shift parade ground while they saluted their countries flag. Then we were marched off to work on the various plantations from dawn till dusk.

One morning I was summoned to see the Japanese officer in command of the garrison. A burly sergeant frog- marched me into his office, saluted, then stood to attention as he pointed at me. Standing there with my head bowed low in front of his superior officer hardly able to breathe, trembling limbs, my nerves torn to shreds, frantically trying to stop my hands shaking as he began interrogating me. He asked me my name in broken English and what I was doing there.

Answering the officer's questions as best I could and explaining to him that I had been hired by a British company as an interpreter for it's foreign labour force. My name was Naomi and I was born in India.

His eyes looked like lifeless glass marbles as he glared at me and he yelled out, "This devil cat ,what kind of animal is she?"

Looking at him the mere sight was beginning to make me shake and tremble all over as I tried to contain my fear. Answering him in a voice trembling with emotion. "She's a family pet, a full grown female Tiger. When you bombed our town you hit the enclosure she was kept in setting her free".

At those last few remarks, he went berserk striking the table with a stick with such force the table began shaking " A family pet, Do you take us for fools or frightened children?. There are no Tigers on these islands".

His latest outrage made my whole being vibrate with fear, explaining as best I could what the Tiger was doing there knowing full well a word out of place would mean instant death.

Those lifeless eyes never left mine as I blurted out my story. He then yelled out an order to the Sergeant, who returned with two more officers. I was immediately taken away and locked in a make- shift bamboo cage with another girl captive. She was a white women named Maria. Her family used to own a plantation on the island until the occupation started.

On the evening of the second day the door was opened and we were both taken out by a company of soldiers and led to a clearing in the jungle. I must have died a thousand times and endured a dozen heart attacks during that short march. My stomach was churning over and over as I dragged my weary body along. It didn't take much working out from the mood of the soldiers we were being taken out into the jungle to be shot.

A piece of land, had been hacked out in the undergrowth making an open space of about fifty yards. At once the guards tied our hands behind us with a short piece of rope, secured to a wooden stake in the middle of the clearing, leaving our legs free so we could at least stand up. Peering through the sweat and tears in my eyes, a camouflaged wooden structure on legs stood behind me. It reminded me of an animal hunting hide. Four soldiers clambered inside and immediately poked two machine gun barrels through the open window. A sergeant lifted my chin up with his stick and in a mocking voice, commented, "let's see if your pussy cat comes for the bait". Yelling out an order he then marched away with the rest of the company leaving me and my fellow captive to the horrors of the night.

It was now getting dark as the jungle took on a sinister look. A full moon made the jungle clearing as light as day. The Japanese where hoping the smell of fear from me and the other captive would entice the Tiger out into the range of their machine gun. Maria and myself were both in a no win situation if 'Suki' didn't get us the machine guns certainly would.

Maria was sobbing bitterly and crying in a hysterical voice as she asked me, 'how will we know when she is here'?. "You won't until it's too late she make's no sound she is a mute'. My voice was choking with fear as I answered her.

Three hours had now passed, the jungle night sounds suddenly ceased, everything went deathly quiet. The dress clinging to my body was soaking wet with sweat I knew in that awful silence my life was hanging on a shoe-string. Death was only seconds away. Crying and shaking hysterically, my poor legs would no longer take the weight of my body as I slumped on my knees to the floor and began praying. "If I'm going to die please make it quick". Normally at night the jungle comes to life with the croaking of bull frogs. Not on this night, straining my eyes to their limits to see into the undergrowth not even a twig or branch moved in that deathly silence.

All of a sudden something big pushed against me and lay down beside me. It's an experience I never want to live through again as slowly I opened one eye then the other.... it was 'Suki'. She was licking her lips blood dripping from them onto the floor. Seeing those huge teeth and claws petrified me with fear, focusing my eyes on her, was I to be her next meal?.

Something inside of me seem to snap as I lapsed into unconsciousness for the next thing I remember I was being awakened by a rifle barrel poking me in the stomach and the sun shining into my eyes. Gazing around me still bewildered the sight in front of me froze the blood in my veins; in the make shift hunting hide, the bodies of two soldiers were half hanging out, their bodies torn to shreds. A pair of lifeless eyes looked straight into mine it was the Japanese sergeant. Yelling out an order for his men to take their dead comrades back to base. One only remaining soldier was told to untie Maria and me. Then the sergeant in a fit of rage gave me a vicious kick on my leg which made me scream out in pain. With almost brute strength he dragged me and Maria by our hair to the edge of the clearing forcing us both to sit on our knees with our heads bowed forward. Sunlight glistened off his razor sharp sword as he drew it back to behead me. In my poor tormented mind kneeling down there I waited in anticipation for the blow that would end my life. It must have seemed like minutes, but Instead his headless bloodstained body fell on the ground next to me still twitching as a huge stripped claw ripped the flesh from his bones sending the blood spurting all over me. His accomplice had ran away to get help. Staggering to my feet still whingeing from the kick on the leg, the huge cat was tearing great chunks of flesh out of the sergeant and eating them. She then stopped and turned her attention to Maria making a bee line for her, who was screeching out in fright and hid behind me. With my arms outstretched behind me to protect Maria I stood very ungainly in front of the big cat. Staring straight into Suki's eyes and shaking my head,

"No Suki no" .... fits of fear were paralysing my whole body even as I spoke. Breathing a sigh of relief I watched as the big cat turned and walked back into the undergrowth. Moments later the soldiers arrived with a young officer pointing to the dead sergeant he asked 'the devil cat.? 'At that moment in time my nerves had gotten the better of me as I yelled at him back. "She is not a devil cat her name is Suki, she's a female tiger, and one day lieutenant we will see what kind of brave man you really are. Instead of bullying poor harmless defenceless women you too will have to face her. My hysterical outburst took him completely by surprise as he yelled out an order to his men, to take us both back to the compound.

Some Australian prisoners of war, twenty in all, had arrived on a supply ship, to help the Japanese improve the harbour defences. They didn't resemble men they were thin and scrawny and the clothes they wore little more than rags, but their tattered appearance had not lost it's funny sense of humour. When hearing about our friendly neighbourhood Tiger terrorising the island they thought it hilarious. At night imprisoned in their compound it was nothing to hear them shouting out aloud. Here, Kitty, Kitty. Meow. Their guards were not amused shouting at them to be silent. This kind of behaviour didn't last long as one day she walked among five of them while they were working on a large man made clean water reservoir. All five clambered and swam into the deeper water and to their sheer horror the big cat followed them in, grabbed one and made off into the bush.

Every morning after parade taking our lives into our hands we walked along those narrow paths to our place of work knowing every step we took could be our last., expecting Suki at any minute to spring from ambush out of dense foliage down the both sides of the path. Some of our guards paid the supreme price by walking too far behind us. We were becoming just like zombies walking so close together you could scarcely put a stick between us but that was the only way to stay alive. During the months that followed, her nightly visits to the enemies compound got more and more daring. It didn't matter what precautions they took she always seemed to be two steps ahead. While the prisoners quarters were locked and guarded, the soldiers had taken up billets in the bombed out houses in the town. This is a period in my life I wish could be erased for good. Time was of little essence, every day seemed the same as the one before, doing the same old routine day after day, right until the end of time itself, as we hadn't got a clue what was going on. Two of my fellow women prisoners their nerves all on edge, had committed suicide due to the tremendous strain we were all under. Life was bad enough being held prisoners by the Japanese without being stalked by a huge man eating tiger. You could always sense Suki's presence by the deathly silence. She was never more than a few yards away at any given time, just lying there watching and waiting in the shadows. A false move or mistake on anyone's part would result in instant death. Even our guards mingled with the prisoners while we toiled in the fields all day. They too could feel those eyes of hatred-watching and overseeing them. You could imagine eyes staring at you from every bush. Doing our ablutions in a discreet place was completely out of the question we had to make do where we stood.

Even the morale and condition of the soldiers in the garrison was at it's lowest point. Using the cover of night, the Tiger was even taking it's prey from the very rooms they occupied. You could hear the nervous gunfire especially at night as the soldiers were firing at everything that moved in the shadows.

It was on one such night Suki's luck finally ran out, a bullet eventually did find its mark and the cat was fatally wounded. After her demise walking to the plantations every morning was like breathing fresh air for the first time, birds were singing in the trees, monkeys swinging above us from branch to branch. Gunfire could be heard far out at sea in the distance, and friendly aircraft could be seen from time to time flying past our Island. We knew from the attitude of our guards something was a foot. One morning on parade we were told very coldly the war was over and we were no longer prisoners. A month later now that things were beginning to get back to normal Suki's decomposed remains were found quite by accident. by some workmen clearing a pathway through the undergrowth. A memorial service was arranged immediately to honour a much loved friend. As people from the towns and villages on the island lined up in their hundreds to pay their last respect. Tears were flooding down my face as I watched the box containing her last remains being slowly pulled on a cart past me for burial.

On a clear winter's morning in 1945 a warship arrived to take what was left of the Japanese garrison off the Island for repatriation. I was given a message that a Japanese officer would like to see me before he left. There was no more arrogance or swagger. I was met with a humble bow and he asked in a quiet voice,

"The devil cat , Is she dead?".

Answering him in a calm and collective voice I replied, "Yes....she is".

"Since the occupation of this island," he continued, "she has claimed the lives of fifty nine of my country men".

The figures were unbelievable. When he told me, I was astounded by that piece of news. I knew she had killed eight prisoners.

This time my tone was very hostile as I answered him back once more "You came to our Island uninvited, killing our people. Through your acts of aggression and brutality, you have made our lives a living hell, and turned a lovable family pet into a man- eating killer. You don't deserve pity, You deserve all you've got, now go and don't ever come back".

Bowing his head as I chastised him he slowly turned and walked away.

Watching all the Japanese soldiers being escorted along the quay side then board the awaiting warship some gave a sigh of relief as they boarded. Seeing the smoke from it's funnel slowly disappearing over the horizon. I breathed a sign of relief: That's one episode in my life that will leave it's scars for all eternity.

A special stone plaque was made for Suki's place of honour in our churchyard, reunited and buried next to the family who loved and cared for her when she was only a small cub. Her name is a legend in itself and will live on in the hearts of the people of this island until the end of time . Her lone fight against an unscrupulous enemy kept the flame of freedom burning, during those dark days of captivity. Her very presence sent tremors of fear through friend and foe alike. Even now when you mention her name you can feel a warm glow of pride fill your whole body. Many of her exploits when told now can be largely exaggerated. Only people who lived then know the truth.

Watching and waiting with baited breath, we saw the tears of emotion running down Naomi's cheeks as she finished her astonishing story. Reaching over to a shelf at her side, she pulled out an old black and white photograph, pointing at the picture.."There.. that's Suki when she was a cub. and the little girl holding her is Rebecca".

Shaking her warmly by the hand I bade an emotional farewell to Naomi thanking her for the time spent in sharing with us that remarkable story. Walking back up the road to our hotel, it's surprising the way a story can play funny tricks with your mind. We could swear something was watching us from the trees.......

THE END

THE WINGED DOG MITES OF BHYKTOR

After spending years on a drawing board, gathering dust, the plans for a new road had been approved and it was now under construction. An ambitious project, the widening of a small track into a two lane major road, across a valley of rocks and crags with a strange grey mist hugging the ground. Mountains rose up on both sides running parallel along the full length of the ten mile long valley . Earth moving equipment had been transported to the region and the contractors were busy tearing and clawing away at any obstacles that lay in the new roads path. Other road building vehicles were in constant use following on behind laying hard core and tarmac for the new road surface. In this part of the world, with its rocky crags, bogs, and dark forests, it was like a place time had forgotten. An old ruined cottage stood, barely visible in the white mists, hanging low over the ground, where someone long ago had tried to make a living, out of this bare and desolate wilderness. Even the trees in the woods seemed stunted in growth due to the harshness of the region. Cruel biting cold winds were tunnelled into the valley by the mountain peaks. Sheets of rain fell relentlessly down breaking branches and felling trees.

Carrying out their allotted tasks day by day the construction workers were experiencing varying degrees of temperatures in this no-man's-land. Plans for this new road had been submitted by different companies, and the successful one was now completing phase one and phase two of the contract. It had been decided to start the thirty mile stretch of road from both ends leaving the ten miles in the middle till last. Pain-staking digging and clawing at the huge rocks and boulders had now started in earnest on the last stretch, clearing away rubble, filling in bogs that could gobble a man up, cutting down trees, was all proving to be much harder than expected as men and machines were constantly breaking down. Up until this moment in time, with favourable weather conditions and a two shift system in operation, the project was well in front of schedule. This was a good sign as huge bonuses would be paid to the workers if the road was finished on time.

However in this valley region between the mountain ranges was turning into a disaster zone as new problems had to be solved each day. Earth moving equipment and diggers that were racing and clearing the ground in record time at the start of the project, were barely coping with a few yards a day. This particular stretch of the road had taken on a new and frightening look. By day the work force faced bitter cold winds and driving rain. As the night fell, grey mists that had been hugging the ground in the day began to rise up, and shadows seem to move in the mist and voices could be heard. Even the staunchest of men in the construction team were getting the jitters and refusing to work on the evening shift. Things were going from bad to worse as workman deserted their jobs and fled in terror, believing the area to be haunted and possessed by the devil. To try and remedy their now dramatic situation more and more men were hired to try and push the project through. Accidents were beginning to be an every day occurrence. One workman spoke out in defence of his work mates at a site meeting and said he had worked on building projects of this nature all around the world. He then described the present situation, ...' Working in the daylight hours was bad enough but as the darkness descended your eyes started imagining the mist taking on ghostly shapes, heads began to appear having holes where their eyes and nose should be. They appeared to be dancing in front of you, low whispering voices came out of nowhere. It was a nerve racking experience, just like working with the dead.'

If that turn of events wasn't bad enough even more bad news

143

reached the sight office one day; they had run into an underground tunnelled complex with stone stair-cases going down into the bowels of the earth and the stench coming out of it was was appalling. Maps of the area were taken out and studied but this installation wasn't shown on any of the regional maps; the whole road building project came grinding to an abrupt halt , as the men flatly refused to go on any further. News of the discovery gave the reporters from the press a field day on hearing the story. They were selling thousands of newspapers all around the world telling of the horrors of the night and being haunted by ghostly apparitions. Stories of this magnitude were also making headlines in all the national newspapers.

A special board meeting had been convened in the road building site office. Engineers were walking about shaking and scratching their heads trying to find a solution to their present dilemma and a way around it. How can you finish a road project when the area is haunted by a supernatural power?.

A young girl telephonist suddenly bursts through the door into the site office very excited and waving her hands. "A man has just telephoned me who knows all about the mysterious underground complex and will be arriving by car to talk to us in the morning!".

Members of the construction board looked at one another in disbelief. Could this be true could he shed some light on their present predicament and help them in what was now a no go area?.

They were waiting patiently in the site office the following morning, twiddling with pencils and talking amongst themselves, and at the stroke of ten, their mysterious guest appeared. A wheelchair was slowly pushed through the door into the room revealing a grey haired old man. A red and green woollen blanket wrapped around his waist and lower parts of his body. Every-ones attention in the room was suddenly channelled as their eyes focused upon the old man. Mouths wide open with surprise, they couldn't believe what was now facing them. Their new visitor; an old man in his nineties if he were a day, his face wrinkled with age, long wisps of grey hair hanging over his shoulders, and a bald head that rebounded the glare of the lights in the room. He wore thick glasses and was trying to focus hard in his new surroundings. A woollen scarf worn around his neck had been knitted in a host of pretty colours, and this was dragging along the floor. His old brown sports coat was full of creases hadn't seen an iron in years.

His shirt, tie and jumper had also seen better days.

Looking at one another in amazement, the board members thought there must be some mistake. Was this someone's idea of a joke?. Was this grey haired old man, the person they had waited all morning to see?. A nurse accompanied him and pushed his wheel chair. She too was no spring chicken, with curly snow white hair hanging down from her nurses cap onto her starched blue uniform. Holding her hand up in the air she addressed the board members there present.

"Gentlemen this is Professor Jonathan Llewelyn from England".

Everyone around the table had their eyes transfixed on the old man. You could hear a pin drop on the floor, as they waited for him to speak. His accent didn't match his attire, he spoke with a beautiful clear voice.

" My name is Professor Jonathan LLewelyn. looking at me now I'm a mere shadow of what I used to be. During the second world war my work as a bio- chemist kept me very busy carrying out experiments in germ warfare, involving the dangers of a possible biological war. In the last few weeks of hostilities alarming news reached our laboratory in a secret location in the London area. A woman wearing a white doctors coat had been found wandering about in a terrible distressed state in this region where we are now. Her whole body covered in huge sores and blisters and she was terribly disfigured. She explained to her captors she knew me from the past and demanded an audience with me at once and as there wasn't a second to lose. It was clearly a matter of life or death".

Her symptoms were described to me over the telephone and immediate action was then taken. I was flown out to the battle zone area. Special quarters had been set up and the poor unfortunate wretch placed in a sealed glass isolation chamber. Interviewing this strange looking women, she didn't resemble any human being I had ever seen before. Bulging eyes four times the size as normal dominated her face, a long thin whispery nose, her mouth was all swollen and out of shape. Pointed ears were standing up straight on the sides of her head. She had rotting black teeth, and bare arms were protruding from tears in a white coat that she wore. They were covered in odious huge weeping blisters and she was completely bald but for a few strands of black matted hair. Alarm bells began ringing in my brain. My biggest nightmare fears were fast turning into a reality, as she bragged openly about a super bug that had been discovered and experimented on, that could wipe out man-kind.

Speaking to this poor woman in this make-shift isolation chamber was beginning to turn my stomach. As the saliva was dripping out of her mouth onto the floor her whole body was twisted and bent out of shape. Her bones were protruding through her skin everywhere, and even as she spoke her mouth being badly swollen meant I had great difficulty in understanding. Two more men had now joined me to make notes and try and get some sense out of this bizarre creature.

"I felt sick inside at the very sight of her and called a halt to the whole proceedings, and went to walk away. However her next sentence stopped me dead in my tracks".

"You don't recognise me, do you Jonathan?".

Hearing my name spoken by a stranger, suddenly all of my thoughts were concentrated on this poor pathetic figure.

Putting her long thin bony hands on the glass widow she spoke again. "Jonathan my name is Doctor Helen Baur. We spent a lot of time wining and dining all those years long ago before the war when we attended university together, discussing and arguing about the important items in our profession. I was a very attractive and desirable woman then".

Looking at this poor pathetic creature in front of me made the tears trickle from my eyes, for I couldn't recognise, the vision of beauty that had attracted me ten years ago. Explaining herself more thoroughly she went on, "Jonathan " every word coming out of her mouth made her body twist in agony.

"At the beginning of the war there was a clamp down on undesirables and intellectuals and we were rounded up in our thousands and was forced to work for the Nazis. Together with two hundred more we were transported to a building complex under construction that went down into the bowels of the earth. It reminded me of a huge maze, caves, tunnels, staircases and rooms all carved out of the rock. It was designed and built with one thing in common, utmost secrecy. Five different levels interlinked by tunnels and stairways; providing access, to living quarters, laboratories, operating theatres, and glass observation chambers to keep test specimens in. Dormitories on the third level held twenty bunk beds in each and housed the workers. All prisoners used for experiments were kept in cells on the bottom levels.

Generators pumping away day and night supplied us with power for lighting and essential equipment. Guard rooms and sentry posts were situated at regular intervals on different levels and manned entirely by civilian personnel wearing different coloured coats to denote their position and rank. Food was stored in specially refrigerated rooms, and large metal tanks held our water supplies. There were Iron doors below ground level that were large enough to let a small lorry pass through, at the end of a short incline, was the only entrance.

"In utmost secrecy in this underground labyrinth, scientists were working on a special project called 'The Winged Dog mites of Bhyktor'. Our project leader was a Professor Hans Ghel, a charismatic, tall well built man, with a Charlie Chaplin moustache, thick brown spectacles hiding a pair of blue piercing eyes,and balding grey hair parted in the middle. With his vast knowledge of bio chemistry had persuaded his superiors to grant him sufficient funds to research deeper into this tiny micro organism.

While doing his daily inspection one morning our paths

crossed, where upon he invited me to accompany him outside for a guided tour. Pointing at a domed shaped building barely visible above the grey mist, only yards from the main entrance "There my dear doctor", pointing at the dome and smiling, "in there lies the answers to all our questions from the past". A quotation he then read above the door sent the shivers racing down my spine.

HE WHO SOWS THE SEEDS OF EVIL.--- WILL REAP ITS VENGEANCE IN FULL.

Everywhere, in any direction was complete desolation. A dirty grey mist rose two feet above the ground, and what plant life there was, seemed to be stunted in growth. Pine trees dominating the region were all bent and twisted. Never in my whole life have I experience a place like this before. The mere sight of it frightened me half to death. His next suggestion sent the blood rushing around my body as he grabbed my arm and led me down some steps into the dirty grey mist. Through a partly opened thick oak door we went inside the strange domed building. Inside it's dark grey walls were ten tombs, stone effigies had been carved on top of each one denoting the family line. It was a mausoleum. Cables passing across the floor provided electric lighting but even that couldn't hide the sheer horror inside. Scores of skeletons were hanging off chains on the walls. These I was informed were grave robbers. Voices coming up from a square staircase on the side belonged to a man holding a powerful light on a lead. His whole actions indicated he had found something of vast importance in the catacombs below. Very reluctantly I followed behind Professor Ghel down the stone steps into a vast honeycomb of catacombs. Here again skeletons were hanging from chains decorating the walls, and the awful smell of death was overpowering. Underground chambers were full of oblong shaped stone tombs all with stone carvings on them. In one part the entrance into the chambers had been bricked up and a white cross pointed on the stone. Behind these forbidden walls entombed for all eternity were the plague victims. As we proceeded deeper into the catacombs we climbed down another flight of stone steps which seemed to go on for ever, leading into a white painted cave. On it's walls were painted bat like insects and big bold words painted in red. 'The Winged Dog Mites Of Bhyktor ',

He whosoever breaketh the seal on the jars will face their wrath.

Three men were busy breaking down a bricked up wall leading into a dark gloomy chamber and inside by the light from the lamps I could see three large stone jars about the height of a twelve year old child.

Professor Ghel then began telling me the reason for our presence there. "During the war's in the holy lands, ten knights were returning back home by sea, and in a freak thunder storm their ship was blown off course forcing them to take refuge in a bay on a remote island. After repairs to their ship they decided to explore the island and to their amazement a stone town containing many houses and a large church had been built in the centre of the island. However not a solitary person or animal walked the streets, it was a ghost town. A bell ringing in the old church made them investigate the new domain further. Ringing the bell was a very old man with a long white beard who explained to them the reason for the lack of human beings and animals. Fifty years ago a casket containing precious stones was taken deep down into the caves under the church. Left to guard this precious treasure trove was a swarm of deadly flying mites. Three young children one day ventured down into the depths of the caves to retrieve some of it's priceless trinkets only to get infected and spread the virus around the island. The children for their dastardly crime were placed alive in three stone jars and then taken down into the depths of the cave. Lids were placed on the jars to trap the mites, hoping the smell of warm blood from the three young bodies would entice them inside. The trap was set then executed and then the tops sealed for all eternity. People of the island paid a terrible price for the children's crime as one by one they became infected. Bodies had to be burnt alive, and also any animals to stop the outbreak spreading. To see a person infected by this strange mite was a devastating experience as his or her body began to reshape into something undescribable. He made all the knights swear an oath by kneeling down and kissing their swords to guard, 'The Winged Dog Mites Of Bhyktor', to the end of time itself. They were to take the three jars from the island and bury them deep in the caves in the cold climates of the countries they came from. In exchange for their acts of chivalry a casket of precious stones would be given to them. However they were warned, that the mites that were imprisoned in these jars. Only three things have kept them trapped in the underworld. One a bright light, two was extreme cold, and finally, three was the fear of fire. When deciding on a location to bury these jars they were to make sure it had all three. At a future date If someone were foolish enough to open the jars and release 'The Winged Dog Mites of Bhyktor' it could spell disaster for the world, it would be destroyed by an epidemic out of control.

This strange mite enters into the blood steam by burying into the skin and laying thousands of eggs and during this period the body goes through a dramatic change becoming twisted and deformed. Once the skin starts to break death his near, the body goes cold and heat can no longer sustain them they will leave the body in their thousands infecting any warm blooded creature they come in contact with.

After returning home from their travels the ten knights honoured their pledge to the old man and built this mausoleum in this desolate region which was partly hidden under-ground, with the three jars buried deep in caverns in the bowels of the earth below. One by one the knights died each one in turn was entombed in the mausoleum to stand guard over, 'The Winged Dog Mites of Bhyktor' for eternity. The last remaining knight suffered from the pangs of fever and let it slip about the jars and the sacred oath given by the ten knights. No one though, has ever dared to venture into this forbidden region until now."

If that story wasn't enough to frighten you half to death now came the biggest bomb shell of all, As he started explaining the reason for us being there and our mission. "Our task is' he went on, " to open those three jars in controlled laboratory conditions and harness the power of, 'The Winged Dog Mites of Bhyktor', from behind sealed glass doors and windows".

Looking at him my body would not stop shaking with fright, "after all the warnings you intend opening the jars". I responded.

Sneering and laughing at me he said, 'Where's your spirit of adventure, by solving the mysteries from the past we can secure our destinies for the future"

Those three earthenware jars had been buried for hundreds of years and it seemed impossible for anything to survive for that length of time. Yet after the lids had been removed by volunteers they arose up like a black cloud. There were literary millions of them. Under a microscope's examination they resembled tiny furry little bats. Over the next few years experiments were carried out in their hundreds with devastating effects. Once the cycle of life had started it was unstoppable, even after death the mites could breed and multiply in a persons dead body leaving it at will. Another frightening episode had also started on breaking the seals and opening the jars. It had awakened the guardians, the ten knights, from their slumber. The whole complex became a gigantic haunted house of horror, accidents and suicides were an every day occurrence. Dark moving shadows and voices whispering were everywhere.

About a month ago there was a mysterious explosion one morning, ripping out walls, glass doors and panels, which released the mites into the lower levels. All the deaths and casualties down there stood little chance from that deadly swarm . In the mayhem that followed all the doors on different levels were locked except the big iron doors at the entrance. They were left partly open to let the fumes out. This was my ideal chance to escape in all the confusion".

"Jonathan I haven't got long promise me when I draw my last breath everything even me in this isolation chamber, you will douse in petrol and burn immediately. Under no circumstances enter and touch my body. For even as we speak 'The Winged Dog Mites of Bhyktor', are breeding in my body at an alarming rate. At my death it will be a signal to them to leave my body in their hundreds and infect other human beings and the result will be an epidemic out of control!."

"Tests carried out on these mites over the passing years show the only way to destroy them is fire and salt water. The period of infection lasts about twenty eight days resulting in a torturous and painful death. As you can see by looking at me, it's not a pretty sight.

" Jonathan please! ....There isn't a moment to lose, that installation must be destroyed and everything in it burned then buried. Nothing must be left alive..... I repeat Jonathan.... NOTHING.. Promise me this on my dying breathe. Gas masks and protective clothing are a must, if anyone gets wounded in the tunnels in that installation his body must be burned immediately. Don't bring anything out of there alive to the surface is that understood ?."

" It's location of what I can remember, about twenty miles from here near a small town called Oustbrook. You will know it when you see it, a valley runs through a mountain range you can't see the floor for mist. There's an old ruined cottage in all this desolation, that is exactly two miles from the entrance.

Be very careful how you approach ! The installation is well guarded. If it's any consolation a blanket of fog hugs the ground and rises up between two and three feet. This you can use as cover to get within attacking distance, but be on your guard, the whole area is rigged with booby traps. I know this from personal experience of other inmates who have tried to escape."

"I suddenly felt the glass vibrate as Helen's finger nails clawed deep marks in it, and her lifeless body slowly went sliding down to the floor".

"There was no time lost in finding the location on our maps. An assault team was quickly assembled which comprised of sixty men and two officers. Secrecy was of the essence if we were to achieve our goal. I was given a crash course in parachuting, unarmed combat, and small arms and in a matter of hours we were flown out into the combat area."

" We landed safely about eight miles from the proposed target, to reconnoitre the area then work out a plan of attack.

Half crawling, half walking, we made our way through a mist shrouded valley approximately one and a half miles wide in amongst the stunted fir trees, bogs and quick sands. With every step, there was the dread of stepping on a mine or trip wire.

There was an eerie stillness about the whole area-enough to give you the creeps. A strange mist hovered above the ground. It was tinted with a funny colour and had a strange smell. Taking no chances seeing as we had come this far without incident, I wasn't going to let anything spoil it now. I gave the order to the men to put on their gas masks.

We stumbled upon a small mountain path with traces of newly worn tyre tracks and decided to follow it, hugging the sides every inch of the way".

"Suddenly the path seem to disappear underground. We heard voices so we knew then that we had found our target. Now came the hard bit: getting inside".

" We decided to split up and investigate our new terrain, in teams of five, gathering all the information we could about our present environment. Notes and sketches were collated together and a battle plan drawn up with the intention of attacking the installation at sunrise the next morning. One of our teams had found the exhaust stack for the generator. This we intended blocking up, and using the fumes to drive our quarry out into the open. Machine gun posts,were also found; these also had to be dealt with.

" Bob Jarvis a ginger haired stocky man, the assault teams C O, made it clear to a young lieutenant and two men, not to let me out of their sight. They were as nervous as me on that late spring morning as we inched forward towards the opening. You can spend hours, days, even months and years planning an operation, and then in the twinkling of an eye it can go all pear-shaped- but not so in our particular case".

The iron doors described by Helen Baur in her dying breath, which we feared so much, were wide open. A small lorry at this very moment in time was being driven out . Nudging the C O ,I spoke in barely a whisper," It's now or never!. We shall never get

153

an opportunity like this again".

"Using the cover of the mist we got as close as possible and then launched our attack. All hell broke loose as bullets were buzzing around over our heads like a swarm of angry bees. The battle for that labyrinth of underground tunnels and rooms had began in earnest. By the sheer surprise of the attack we had captured the generator room intact so instead of groping about in the darkness we could see our targets. Flame throwers and grenades pushed the defenders deeper into that maze of corridors and caves".

"As we got deeper into the complex looking through the surviving sealed windowed rooms the extent of their experiments, was becoming very clear to me.

Men women and children in various stages of the virus were imprisoned in these glass dungeons so that they could be monitored for experimental reasons. It made my stomach turn over then, and still does now when I think about It."

"Reaching the bottom level, the stench was unbearable; bodies lay strewn across the floors in the various rooms, I remembered the last words spoken to me by Doctor Helen Baur: Everything most be burnt and destroyed in that building, Nothing must survive".

"All resistance had now been crushed and we were in charge. I asked the C O to get his men to take all available petrol from the generator plant and pour it down into the tunnels, rooms and caves. Then to set explosives as this whole underground building complex, including the mausoleum, must be obliterated and buried".

Walking back up the ramp through the mist to the top, my mind seemed numb and paralysed with fear at the shock of what I had just witnessed. I couldn't get my thoughts together".

Just then one of the directors interrupted Jonathon's story,

"How big approximately is the underground building".

Jonathan answered him sarcastically,

"When you're groping your way down a corridor trying to blend your body into the concrete walls, bullets whistling all around you, the last thing you want to do, is take out a tape and measure the dimensions".

This remark was hailed with a roar of laughter from the board.

The director apologised and insisted Jonathan continue his story.

" Sitting at the top of that incline for what seemed to me like an eternity vibrations from explosions below where the assault team were systematically blowing up and sealing off the tunnels on the different levels, the noise was making the whole ground shudder. Alarm bells began ringing in my mind.... We had caught the enemy lorry coming through the open door; what if the operation was finished and it had all been rigged with explosives to be detonated by a timing device on their departure?. The thought had barely entered my mind when the whole ground lifted up, fire and flames shooting up everywhere. Something sharp embedded itself in the top part of my leg. Trying to stand up, my leg just gave way. Watching and waiting in all that carnage will live in my mind until the day I die. No one emerged from the tunnels. Young lads who only hours a go had been laughing and joking, had all gone. Dragging my battered and broken body in that wilderness for what seemed like miles,until an allied patrol finally picked me up.

For the next thing I remember was being awakened one morning in a hospital bed and told gently my left leg had been amputated. A doctor wearing civilian clothes then began filling me in on all the gory details. My biggest shock of all; it was Christmas Eve,1945. All the many injuries I had sustained had caused amnesia blocking out part of my life.

Jonathon's story had held the board members spellbound as he described the various incidents in the campaign. Now came the punch line".

" Gentlemen, you have all worked extremely hard on this road project. 'The Winged Dog Mites of Bhyktor' have claimed hundreds and probably thousands of innocent lives. What I'm about to say to you is the whole area is like one gigantic burial ground so let the dead rest in peace. You have ways and means at your disposal, so alter the route of your road and go around the underground laboratory, and let sleeping dogs lie".

Jonathon's talk was heralded with a host of loud cheers as he finished.

THE END

157

158

T LYNDON &
MARIAN

BEST WISHES
FOR
2011
RAY
B.T Edwards

160